PLUMMET AND SHINE

AND OTHER STORIES

JOAN KORALE

NFB
Buffalo, New York

Copyright © 2017 Joan Korale

Printed in the United States of America

Plummet and Shine and Other Stories/ Korale- 1st Edition

ISBN: 978-0-9988811-2-6

1.Plummet and Shine. 2. Short Stories. 3. Jamaica. 4. Hawaii.
5. Military. 6. Collection. 7. Korale.

This is a work of fiction. All characters ~~in this novel~~ are fictitious. Any resemblance to actual events or locations, unless specified, or persons, living or dead is entirely coincidental.

No part of this book may be reproduced or transmitted in any form by any means, electronic or mechanical, including photocopying, recording, or by any information storage and retrieval system without permission in writing by the
author.

NFB
<<<>>>
NFB Publishing/Amelia Press
119 Dorchester Road
Buffalo, New York 14213

For more information visit Nfbpublishing.com

To Ruth, my beautiful mother,
who insisted I take typing

And

To Elizabeth Cotten (with an e),
who turned her guitar upside down
to play left-handed and
wrote a haunting song

CONTENTS

MAINLAND
Legacy 9
Jersey Devil 27
Kindness of the Cook 35
Burnt Sienna 45
Miracle at Black Rock 51

JAMAICA
Compass 61
Designated Smoking Area 81
Riding the Train with Claude McKay 89

HAWAII
Site-Faithful 97
Tapping the Pocket Mirror 113
The Green Umbrella 133

MILITARY
Sankshuery 143
Runaway Train 149
Plummet and Shine 157
Rings 185

*"...Man's little works, strewn on the sands of time,
sparkle like cut jewels in the beatitude of God's countenance."*

~ Robert Bridges

MAINLAND

Legacy

The Burris brothers, Porter and Josh, inherited a dog breeding business on the death of their father. For Porter, the elder brother, it was a part-time concern as he made his living alongside his father-in-law cleaning septic tanks. Even so, when pressed by his younger brother, Porter only reluctantly relinquished legal ownership to Josh for whom breeding pure-bred boxer pups was a full-time job, his livelihood, a calling. Now sixty something, Josh, single, sick, and childless, wanted the business to outlive him, but only if the life and death changes he initiated were honored.

Legacy

Born partially deaf, Josh suffered a sporadic speech impediment and could hardly read. School being torture, he dropped out at sixteen. He worked very hard over the years as a specialty dog breeder and at being a handy-man and had created a viable business to leave an heir. Josh telephoned Lara, his niece, who was seventeen and about to graduate high school and asked to meet with her. She was the natural candidate to take his place. Without any word to the family, Josh had drawn up a will.

Lara did love the dogs. She and her uncle spent happy hours grooming them at the kennel and running the dogs along the beach to roust about in the waves in Ocean City or Wildwood. Before high school, Lara hung out at the kennel every day. "Nothing's changed," Josh convinced himself. "After graduation, she'll have the time again."

For Lara to assume responsibility, she and Josh would have to butt horns with her father who, to Josh's thinking followed inhumane practices, and her mother, Pattie, who fought any idea that wasn't hers. Josh could hear them, "Lara's a girl. She's way too young. We'd be doing all the work. She hasn't got the heart to euthanize." Josh knew that much was true, and he was glad for it.

Most Jersey teenagers, primed by its alluring proximity, long to polish the Big Apple, so Josh wasn't surprised when Lara suggested they meet for Saturday brunch at Prunella's Roost, "a bistro," she said, east of midtown Manhattan. She'd found it on Yelp, wanted to check it out, and, although she didn't tell her Uncle, deemed it remote enough that she wouldn't encounter high school friends. For Josh's part, he'd be reminiscing his wolf pack days.

In the year or two before Josh reached legal drinking age in New Jersey, he, his brother, and a posse of friends emerged on weekends from musky Jersey pinelands in a reclaimed wreck of a rusted '55 Ford 100 pick-up to prowl Manhattan like young wolves into tavern dens. These days Josh had developed a raucous cough, a bulging belly that weighed him down, and a bum knee from kneeling over his pups. He *could* claim with pride a current model Ford pick-up.

Josh arrived at Prunella's Roost first. The trip had worn him down more than anticipated. Sipping coffee assumed medicinal importance. The waitress, a quick and tidy middle-aged model of efficiency labeled Kathy on her apron with a pencil behind one ear, brought his coffee in a small French press.

"What the hell is that?" Josh looked at her. "Excuse me--heck."

Without a word, Kathy lifted and pushed the plunger down in slow motion, poured the resulting brew into Josh's mug, and left. She soon returned with iced water because, despite the chill outside, Josh appeared overheated. "Best cup of coffee, huh, ever," Josh raised the glass mug. "I'm glad for it." Most expensive, too, he thought. Whooee.

Josh grinned at the dainty round metal ice cream table covered with purple gingham. He snorted a laugh and placed the gift he brought for Lara on a seat beside him. His mother might have been proud of him. Lara was named after his mother after all and looked like her, his father often insisted. Josh savored the "Chiapas Organic Coffee Especial." For sure Josh's dad and brother wouldn't have paid this much for anything that wasn't 12% alcohol. Josh was different from habit.

He was the family's orphan uncle who attended holiday dinners solo. This Thanksgiving he did invite Bea, who endured the smothering compulsion of everyone to marry

Josh off and the probing questions.

"How do you stand riding in that truck with the boxers," his sister-in-law asked. "They drool and stink so."

Was it the family's or the boxers' fault Bea hadn't returned calls? He was pretty sure Bea lost interest when he told her what the doctor said.

Josh squirmed. Never a reader, he had only thoughts to wait with. He sure would prefer to have one of his dogs along. Josh loved his boxers. They formed a frame for his life in lieu of a wife and children.

Josh had learned a lot about the breed. His fawn-coloreds and the brindles would sell, but hardly anyone who knew anything about boxers wanted the whites. Josh's father and brother drowned the white pups, which Josh did with the first yield of two whites in one litter of eight. He winced. Pretending to wipe his mouth, Josh blotted his eyes with a napkin and grunted.

He'd tried to do right since then, hadn't he? To save future whites, Josh visited every dog rescue within hundreds of miles. In the next state over near a vast Veteran's Hospital complex he discovered Zoe at Precious Paws and Purrs. Predominant among rescues were abandoned declawed cats and white boxers.

Josh described Zoe's clean and ample shelter to Lara as "a piece of white dog heaven." Josh commiserated that although they are a normal representation of their breed, not albinos, a large percentage of whites are born deaf. Zoe who already knew that, had discovered that white boxers had talent as therapy dogs.

Zoe taught him that whites could learn after one trip the directions to church or the supermarket or the doctor, and inside the home could fetch blankets, newspapers, even the telephone or a neighbor in the event of a fall.

Josh grinned, fiercely proud of the whites, his service dogs. He warmed his coffee from dregs in the press.

In these his older years Josh kept Felicity, a small, solid, spotted white for himself. "I'm deaf, she's deaf, we're twins." Josh made Zoe promise that if anything happened to him, she would fetch Felicity. He flipped open his cell phone to see that he had Zoe's number under "EMERGENCY Call," as he'd instructed the family. Josh figured Felicity to be nearly Lara's age in people years.

A little over two and a half years ago on a star stitched moonless night, after pacing the wilds surrounding his cabin with a mag light, Josh discovered Dina, his favorite at the time, giving birth in the pine needle carpeted hollow of a gnarled pitch pine within the barrens. The bitch whimpered, her labored breaths huffing cloudlets that painted the flashlight wet. Josh unwrapped a fleece blanket warmed with a Clorox bottle of hot water and rolled her onto it. Then he kneeled by her and prayed. If there was a white in this litter he'd own it. He stayed awake to watch Dina deliver four pups before she rasped and her breathing stopped. In the blanket warmed by their mother Josh sheltered the pups, including Felicity.

Now he, Josh, was succumbing to blockage of breath. He glanced at a poster advertising live music. He recalled a folksinger who had lung cancer and repeated a line of the songwriter's last song.

"You gave me your heart, Would you give me your lungs?"

The stalwart waitress heard something. "More coffee?"

"Huh, sure."

She replaced one French press with another. Overkill, Josh thought. "Maybe you folks need a bigger coffee pot. Thanks on yah though," he said.

    The waitress paused, "You waiting for somebody?"

    "Yeah, huh, my niece—a teenager."

    "Teenagers. They're on their own clocks."

    "She'll come. This was her, huh, idea."

    "Yup. Of course it was her idea."

She had to show up. Josh wanted, desired, to forge a legacy. Lately, a knife sharp pain split his knee as he rose from bed in the morning chill and dark to mix meal for the boxers. He took to leaving their bowls out at night in spite of apprehension that a coyote or raccoon might forage. For Josh, drawing breaths became at times, especially in the black hole of night, an alarming chore.

    Josh took a deliberate breath, his eyes settling on ice pieces like tiny rafts of amethyst in his glass. He dipped three fingers and lifted two of the ice jewels to his mouth. A bangled and pantsuited girl at the next table eyed him with disdain, but the ice tasted sweet.

    About to yield to the sudden sharp urge for a cigarette, Josh pushed a pack from his T-shirt pocket onto the table. Just then Lara stood in the doorway unfurling a black and white hound's-tooth scarf and glancing around for him. He flipped a wave. Lara nodded carrying inside her brand of the weather's brisk vitality. How she'd grown. He stood while his pretty niece anchored her coat and scarf on the chair, then he leaned too far forward drubbing her with an awkward bear hug.

"Why are we meeting in secret?" Lara teased smoothing back her long sleek hair.

"I need to talk to you. Your mother said last time I stopped over your place, huh, the dogs trampled her flower beds." In truth, Josh didn't want his sister-in-law warbling over his health.

Lara dangled keys, "Daddy lent me the car. First time."

Josh nodded. "He know you were driving into the city?"

Lara's mischievous eyes answered. She waved for the waitress. "I'm starving, but I don't have much time, Uncle Josh. I have to be somewhere."

Lara ordered guava juice and a soy-sausage biscuit. To show off his French press chops, Josh ordered another coffee and a piece of crumb dusted coffeecake, which was a mistake because it set him to coughing, his eyes and nose watering. Josh stood and grasped a pillar.

Lara noticed the pantsuit girl staring. "Have you seen a doctor, Uncle Josh?"

He steadied himself. "Huh, it's just a cold, Darling."

Darling—the word embarrassed Lara and hung in the air like an unwanted cloud of perfume spritzed onto a Mall shopper. Josh collapsed back into his seat his eyes appealing to the teenager for patience. Lara looked past him at a wall clock.

"I have to be somewhere, Uncle Josh, before Dad or Mom misses the car. Thanks for breakfast." She wrapped the rest of her biscuit in a napkin and was already pushing away from the table.

"Just WAIT!" he yelled too loud. Lara, sank back into her chair as if she could sink out of sight of turning heads.

Josh lifted the stashed oval wooden frame onto the table. Lara took and studied it.

"It's me?"

"Another Lara, your Grandmom. And there's more."

Lara said, "Thanks, Uncle Josh, you don't want it?"

Josh bowed his head in frustration. "I want you

to have it—huh. I want to talk to you about something. Important."

"Cool," she said ignoring the second part of his statement, "Thanks, Uncle Josh." Lara stood and hugged him still holding the photo in her fingers. Josh breathed in her perfume (since when did she wear perfume?), helped her on with her coat, and stifled a cough as she turned away. It was no use bringing up the business now. The future of the boxers so crucial to him wasn't a blip on Lara's teenage radar. "Don't be losing that, Lara," he said as she walked away, "it's very important to us."

"To us," caught her attention. Lara turned at the door and waved the photo, "Bye, Uncle Josh, thanks for breakfast. I love you."

"Me, huh, too," Josh managed. "Don't lose it," he said to nobody as the door closed.

The waitress eyeing an accumulation of the shopping and work crowds mewling at the door brought the check ignoring Lara's rude departure.

Befuddled, Josh paid up and numbly tread limping to where he parked his pickup. "Shit." He decided to abandon the cigarettes on the café table, climbed into the pickup and started home. Stop and go, stop and go, "stop and friggin go." He hadn't obeyed this many tightass streetlights in decades. He snailed through a tunnel, and finally picked up speed over a bridge. His chest burning, he managed to wheel his truck into the first rest stop on the Jersey side. In line at the convenience counter, Josh gestured for a mother carrying her baby in a cloth sling to go ahead of him. He then called out to the mirrored sunglasses of a passing security guard, "Bud, how's 'bout a leg up" and collapsed. The baby started to cry.

Lara's mother felt called upon to make arrangements. She telephoned a competitor's kennel to deal with the pick up of three boxers penned at Josh's. She then drove to his house herself and picked up clothes and Josh's house dog, Felicity. She made the "Emergency Call" Josh had planned to Zoe at Precious Paws and Purrs, and, to kill two birds, she arranged to have the exchange of Felicity happen at the funeral home.

"He lived in jeans; he died in jeans." Lara's mom handed a pile of jeans, socks, white cotton briefs and a T-shirt, a plaid flannel shirt and buffed work shoes to the funeral director. "His clothes still stink of dog. He couldn't smell them for the cigarettes."

She had left Josh's white boxer pacing in the back seat of the family car with something clamped in her jaws. Lara's mom didn't want her car soiled and ran back to retrieve whatever Felicity was chawing on before the shelter lady showed up.

Fearful and squeamish of slobber, Lara's mom was deciding what to do when Zoe's Precious Paws and Purrs van arrived. "She's mouthing something," Lara's mom said, then she opened the car door to make the exchange. Felicity darted for the funeral home and leaped scratching at the door.

Lara's mom ran behind, "Felicity. Drop it. Get down. Felicity."

"She can't hear you," Zoe called, striding behind. Before they reached the door, the funeral director opened it. Felicity, still holding the object in her teeth, lightninged past straight to the pile of Josh's clothes in the office on a chair. She darted around the room confused. Zoe, leash in hand, hurried past Lara's mom and the director, petted Felicity and leashed her. She knelt and pushed the pile of

Josh's clothing beneath Felicity's jaws. Felicity dropped the framed portrait of Josh's mother, onto the pile.

"Good girl," Zoe soothed. Zoe looked up at the Funeral director and Lara's Mom. "Can we keep something of Josh's?"

"There's nothing really here," Lara's mother said.

"Here." The funeral director offered Josh's T-shirt.

Lara's mother nodded a weak assent, "Well OK."

"Thank you." Zoe folded the T-shirt under Felicity's collar. "Come sweetness." Zoe coaxed Felicity from the building and into the van. Later, the framed photo of Josh's mother, although the glass had cracked in the fray, was placed according to Lara's mother's instructions "in Josh's coffin near his heart." Lara's mother, in an over-solicitous effort to protect Lara, took an opportunity at the service to distract her. "Oh God, there's the Precious Paws van. I can't believe that woman dragged Felicity here. Go stop her."

Lara reached the van just as Zoe was lowering a young man in a wheelchair. Several abler seniors exited the side doors.

"I'm Josh's niece. Felicity can't come in, please."

"Sorry for your loss. Felicity's at the shelter just as your uncle wished. All of these folks own Josh's whites as service dogs."

"Just came to pay respects," the young man said.

"Sure."

Wondering about her uncle's contributions Lara came back inside and knelt by Josh's coffin. Her mother joined her. "He would have loved that picture. You know it's a photograph of your father's mother, your grandmother. She died giving birth to Uncle Josh," Lara let her mother explain.

For the second time, Lara studied the familiar face.

"Felicity carried it, she must have, from Uncle Josh's house," Lara's mom said. "Like an angel."

"It's broken." Lara said, mesmerized.

"That won't bother Uncle Josh now," her mother said, and she closed her eyes to pray. When she opened them to make the sign of the cross, she gripped Lara's arm reaching for the frame. "Leave it. What are you doing?"

"I can fix it," Lara said.

"I think Uncle Josh should have it as it is," her

mother said taking hold of the frame.

Lara released the photo and walked on legs of rubber to lower herself into a front row seat. She sat and watched as one by one Josh's lady friend, Bea, other family she hardly knew, and the seniors and disabled Vet came forward to say good-bye to her uncle.

Soon the funeral director entered and whispered to Lara's mother who nodded, said another prayer, and backed away after a final sign of the cross. Lara's dad and several male friends strolled forward in a phalanx of purpose. The undertaker unhitched a restraining latch, lowered and let fall the coffin lid.

Lara screamed, "No, WAIT. Please hold on!" She lurched forward. Her mother reached out and caught her arm again.

"It's OK. It's OK," Lara's mother crooned.

"I HAVE to have that photo," Lara stopped sobbing to say. "Uncle Josh gave it to me in New York City."

"You've never been to New York City with Uncle Josh."

"Cool it you two. Lara, let us get on with this." Her father's impatience usually held sway.

"He wanted me to have it."

The undertaker without another word deftly reopened the coffin, signaled with the side of his hand for the pallbearers to stand by, extracted the photo, and handed it to Lara, still in her mother's tight grip.

Lara and her mother backed out of the way and plopped down again in the row of seats. Lara held the photo on her lap. Lara's mom pulled on black wool gloves. The posse of pallbearers hefted the coffin and labored through an opened double door to the yawning hearse.

"I'm sorry Mom," Lara said. She was sorry to have upset her mother on that day, but an older Lara in future accounts she would make of her life's regrets would not include driving the family car into the city to see her uncle, telling him she loved him, calling out for the photograph at his funeral, and taking over the business as ordained in Josh's will, which was discovered folded into the broken frame.

Jersey Devil

Elwood and I hovered over her as Grandmom squinted at the thermometer she pulled from Tom's lips. Shaking the thermometer back to normal she said into our chins, "You two may go on, Tom's feverish."

I banged my fist into the sofa arm. "We'll be practically in the backyard," I said. I wanted my nice cousin along on the camp out. Truth is Elwood bullies me and says I have a yellow streak down my back. I don't.

"Tom's sick, Lucy. He's burning up," Grandmom insisted.

"Only me and Elwood then?"

Elwood yanked on his ball cap and turned to pack up.

"Yes," said Grandmom and Elwood, who heckled over his shoulder, "I'll start the fire, Fraidy-cat."

When we headed out at sunset, Tom, flushed with fever and wearing striped pajamas, waved from the window. In the lighted kitchen, I watched Grandmom chopping chicken for soup. In back, Grandpop gathered dry laundry.

From a long-ago injury, Grandpop's left arm is a twisted stump. This evening, he walked along the clothesline unpinning clothes with his working hand and letting gravity deposit each stiffened garment, towel, and washrag into the oval basket positioned underneath and moved along with a foot nudge. I ran to kiss him as Elwood and I walked past to enter the path into the Pine Barrens.

"Here," Grandpop said, "Take a blanket so's you don't catch Tom's cold." He rolled the blanket around his bad arm, slid it off, and stuffed it through my backpack straps.

He does a lot with that arm. "It's a design feature,

not a flaw," he always says. During the depression, to put food on the table, Grandpop worked as a taxidermist crafting decoys for hunters and farmers. Personally, I don't like the decoys. "Your Grandpop found what work he could," Grandmom says. Uncle Mitch, Elwood's dad, warns us cousins, "Even with that arm, your Grandpop can spank." Truth is I never saw Grandpop hurt anybody. Uncle Mitch makes Elwood's nose bleed, even locked him in a closet once, and seems like at least once every day he calls Elwood a sissy. Grandpop's way kinder.

"Thanks, Grandpop," I said.

He nodded, lifted his chin and called out, "Tend your fire, Elwood."

I ran to catch up with Elwood who was walking briskly on purpose. Evening fell moist and misty. We breathed the piney musk of darkening woods both toting split logs under each arm. "We're lucky it's damp," I huffed, "or Grandpop wouldn't've allowed a fire." Campfires spread too easy when fallen pine needles crisp up.

We stop having selected a clearing. Elwood collects kindling and stones for the fire circle. I whiskbroom a spot for sleeping bags. Under the Christmassy cathedral of pitch pines sounds amplify. From far off I hear branches crack, but already I can't see Elwood for fog creeping in.

At last and after our best efforts our crackling fire pulls the plug on pesky buzz-sawing mosquitoes. Elwood and I draw close to the campfire and sit mesmerized, but idle. The diamond necklaces and ladles of stars I'd wanted to see are obscured by a blindfold of fog. If Tom were here, we'd strum his ukulele and take a shot at figuring out our favorite tunes. Tom and I do that a lot. Elwood not so much cause Uncle Mitch says singing's "for girls and choirboy sissies." Grandmom says music's an angel's echo. From as long as I can remember she'd comfort us to sleep singing old hymns like "What a Friend," or folk songs like "Shenandoah."

"Know how Grandpop hurt his arm?" Elwood asked flatly.

"Yes," I said, and recited the family litany, "He fell from a tree and broke it so bad the doctor threatened to amputate, but Great-Grandpop said, 'Leave it. A stump is better than no arm at all.'"

"Not how it happened," Elwood said staring hard at me.

My mouth was dry. Icy water from my canteen tasted good. I offered Elwood some.

He shook his head. "You know Grandpop's decoys?"

"Sure," I said. Truth is I hate going into the cellar past the staring row of stuffed crows, an owl, mallard ducks, a rabbit, even a fox that came after Grandpop's bantam hens and pigeon squabs.

Elwood kicked in a stray ember, "my dad says a rich man from Philly once offered Grandpop a thousand dollars to catch and stuff the Jersey Devil."

"Grandpop says there is no Jersey Devil."

"He just doesn't want you to be scared. You know anything about the Jersey Devil?"

In school we had to draw a picture once. "It has the head of a goat or horse, bat wings, little arms with hawk talons, crane legs with horse's hooves, and it screeches."

"Yup." Elwood tossed a pinecone into the flames. "Dad says Grandpop and this rich man went gunning, and using Grandpop's decoys, they set traps..."

"Grandpop hates traps. The decoys are lures or scarecrows, that's all."

"Dad says they had it trapped ...," Elwood said, his eyes wild, "...the Jersey Devil. They heard it screeching." Then, Elwood started screeching, "EEEEYA, EEEEYA. EEEEYA."

I stood up. "Stop it, Elwood. I don't like that. STOP IT NOW."

"EEEYA, EEEYA, EEEYA, EEEAHYAAAA."

He stopped cold when we heard or felt something crashing through the underbrush—Thumpah, Thumpah, Thumpah. Elwood bolted up. "Run," he said.

"Hey, you don't leave a fire." I grabbed his shirt and spun him around.

Elwood was startled, and I was relieved when Grandpop appeared panting and flushed.

Right off I told Grandpop, "Uncle Mitch says you trapped the Jersey Devil."

"What?" Grandpop said. "Ha!" He sat down cross-legged and waited till we sat and stopped fidgeting. When Grandpop's serious, he gets everybody quiet, then talks. "An old Lenni-Lenape Indian I know tells it like this," Grandpop said. "Long ago at powwows with wannabe settlers the tribe invented the Jersey Devil story—to spook undesirables."

"Undesirables?" I said.

"Reckless, ignorant, close-minded people. Anybody fired up to strike out and ruin what scares them, what they don't understand."

Elwood stirred embers with a poker of green pitch pine engendering a tiny firework display. Without one other word, Grandpop stood up and started home.

I wanted music. "Be right back." I caught up with Grandpop to borrow Tom's ukulele. Tom was asleep so I only had to lift it from between two pegs Grandpop hung on the wall. On returning, I stood still at the mouth of the Pine Barrens to listen. Sweet unbounded strains of Shenandoah cut through the fog. Elwood. Singing.

KINDNESS OF THE COOK

Reba woke from a dream in which she found, like coming upon a failed cake in the oven, her own self dead. The dream weighed on her and at first made it harder to get up and go in to her new job, until she remembered that in her dream, she, the not dead dreamer, felt grateful to be alive.

Later in the early morning at work, when her co-workers gathered to perform as on occasion they did, Reba pushed the steel mixing bowl to the end of her bake station to better hear Barton, Swooni and Cliff Tom serenade Katharine, their queen of the salad station. The a capella harmony of "People Get Ready" with three sets of fingers snapping and Barton alternately flicking his apron-covered thigh with a ball whisk transformed the sterile steel kitchen into a chantry. Reba closed her eyes to savor Cliff Tom's falsetto spiking high spiraling notes of liquid glass.

Suddenly, door hinges squeaked. Jerry the kitchen foreman strode in and yelled. "Hey. Cut the crap. Back to f'n work deadbeats." He slapped an oily wooden baton full of keys on one of the counters. Several times every day for two weeks, he'd detonated his baton of keys on the steel work counters. Reba felt sparks fly each time even if she didn't see any.

"What all in a restaurant is locked? Why does Jerry need so many keys?" Reba had asked Barton, the dish washer. "They're the idle keys to his personality and manhood," Barton smirked in a voice timbrous and resonantly baritone.

Truth was on this morning no one was slacking off, if that was Jerry's true concern. Queen Katherine the Beautiful, her teeming auburn hair caught in a net, had not stopped chopping lettuce, Reba continued to stir and measure for the daily loaves, Barton had long finished loading the breakfast dish load, and Swooni's line shift had not yet even started. Cliff Tom who had already checked out from the late night shift threw Queen Katharine an unacknowledged kiss and winked good bye. "I'm outta here, Sunshine."

At Jerry's rude key slap, Reba's spoon and measuring cup grew heavier and her legs, arms and hands so very tired. She repositioned her tools and task to be farther away from him, but Jerry snapped his keys on her station to demand eye contact as if she were some animal being trained.

He didn't bother address Reba by her name. "Some regular lunch honcho called in a special cake order. It must be there by 2 p.m. tomorrow."

"I'm off tomorrow, Jerry."

"Switch days. You're on probation remember? Anyhow there might be a big tip in it for you. He's an important client," Jerry said, searching for the right hook. "He says your chocolate layer cake is…," he grimaced," … 'life affirming'."

"Thanks, Jerry."

"Whatever." Jerry pulled a prepared cardboard, string and waxed paper sheath from a slot under the counter. "Here's the take-out packaging. No drivers on tomorrow, so you'll be delivering it."

"I'm off, but I live in town. Pay me for say three hours, I don't have enough for overtime yet anyway, and I'll bake it and take it from home."

Jerry hesitated, but he saw no choice. "Whatever. Here's the address and order. Take what you need out of inventory. Only what you need."

"Whatever," Reba said.

"What?"

"I'll take whatever I need."

"Give me your cell number." Reba recited it and Jerry punched the number into his Blackberry. "I'll call you."

"You don't have to call me, Jerry. Two o'clock. If you want, just text or email me the address for insurance."

"I'm calling you." Already smiling and morphing into a strutting flirt, Jerry glided toward the salad station and pretty Katharine who visibly cowed. Jerry couldn't help glancing at his watch. "Time to restock the salad bar, Sweetheart." He pulled the cart from its niche and started loading.

"I'm on it, Jerry. Thank you." Katharine released a dazzling false smile.

"Good girl." He had to stop himself from touching her, but he didn't stop himself from slapping the counter one more slap on his way out. Katherine and Reba started at the sound.

Close to the end of her shift, Reba entered the supply closet, selected several gold foiled dark chocolate packets, and dropped them into the cloth saddle bag that she carried for a purse decorated with two fried eggs sunny-side-up for the eyes and a curved strip of bacon completing a smiley face. She helped herself to two extra packets of chocolate to sample because she didn't take any flour, and butter was too much trouble to carry in summer. She had better sugar, baking powder and vanilla at home. She did slip four eggs into an empty cottage cheese container cushioning them with paper towel. She may not have enough eggs in her fridge.

To avoid explanation, she had planned to stow ingredients before Mrs. Biaggi's arrival, but when she emerged from the closet Mrs. Biaggi was spraying disinfectant and wiping down the station. Reba had already done that, and thoroughly, but not to Mrs. Biaggi's satisfaction. Reba thought, she's marking her turf like a tomcat.

Mrs. Biaggi leered at Reba's bag, but didn't say anything. In the two weeks since Reba started work, Mrs. Biaggi hadn't bothered to make much small talk although their shifts coincided for one half hour. Reba hadn't worked there long enough to share any bonding experiences, and they couldn't discuss husband, children or grandchildren since Reba didn't have any. Mrs. Biaggi talked more with Katharine. "Don't you look pretty today." Reba wondered if Katharine, with all these outside assurances, avoided the feeling of cloying aloneness. Reba shrugged. Even Katherine has to deal with the Jerrys of this world.

"Bye," Reba announced mostly to Katharine.

"Hey, I'll walk you out." Katharine knew her boyfriend would be waiting for her on the street in his Porsche. He was.

"So long." Katharine called, swinging free her glorious hair as she and the boyfriend sped away not looking back.

Reba bought a newspaper. Job hunting had become

a habit, and continuing to look for a job made this job tolerable. If she left, she would miss only the crooners, certainly she wouldn't miss Jerry. Jerry could jangle his keys and dance on broken glass.

Reba had achieved a culinary degree and her ServSafe Certificate, the necessary cook credentials. Now she wanted nothing less than to electrify her days with purpose. The client found her chocolate cake "life affirming." She wanted her job to be life affirming. This job pretty much sucked, but this was real life, wasn't it?

She opened a new email from Jerry on her phone. Since she was still "on probation," baking this cake would be considered the final stage of the job interview. He'd figured a way to leverage her time. "This company is one of our most distinguished clients," Jerry had copied to corporate to cover his butt. "When it is confirmed that you have delivered this order to the client's satisfaction, we will inform you of our final decision concerning your employment. Deliver the prepaid cake today, wrapped as instructed, to the above address in time for a 2 p.m. meeting. I will telephone you with a reminder."

As she would have done anyway, Reba baked with

passion. The tang of shredded fine dark chocolate, the pilfered sample, thrilled her as it swam away on her tongue. Perfect. Combining the stalwart texture and flavor of fine organic butter and crystals of golden sugar was like marrying Lancelot to Guinevere. The flour brand was King Arthur. She turned the illustration on the bag around so that King Arthur would not interfere with the betraying lovers. The surrender of the mixture at room temperature to the intrusion of her whirling wooden spoon blending the yellow suns and miracle clear clabber of eggs sang to her, as did the flumpf of flour into the earthen bowl, the bowl she loved enough to be buried with. She felt born to manage the exactitude of baking powder and vanilla and the correct size greased tins. She marveled at the chemistry, the role of heat and the steadfast attention to timing that birthed the spring and carriage of her done bread, rolls and cakes.

Reba had just closed her oven door when her cell phone rang. She wiped her hands on her apron. "Hello. I know, 2:00 o'clock, Jerry. I will. I know. Good bye."

He called again after she'd cooled and frosted the cake. "It's done. Yes. I know it's raining. I will."

As she finished up the wrapping she heard a siren in the distance. She put on a poncho raincoat instead of carrying an umbrella; she wanted to protect and caress her cake.

The city was smelly and misty in the rain, as if a great dog huffed the fog onto it, was hovering with fetid breath and had licked the streets slippery. In this oppressive air, the aroma of chocolate exuded like hope. The hood of her raincoat hung out over Reba's face, and she didn't see the blue lights of the police and fire trucks until her feet were sprayed by a swirling fire hose which was washing blood from the sidewalk. She backed away from the hose into the edge of a gathering crowd where an old man caught her in almost a hug. "What happened?"

"Young boy on a bicycle. Hit by a car. I'm thinking critical or worse. Ambulance took him already. Hit and run. Damn. Nobody gives a damn these days. I know the family. Corner house past the dry cleaner."

Her heart beating hard against the protected cake, Reba heard the squeak of the cake box against its string, like a teeny violin. In the midst of the rain there hung in the air a dry salty feeling of irreversible calamity.

Kindness of the Cook

Wearing blue plastic gloves, two policeman , one skinny and very young, one fat, older and flushed with fatigue, picked the crippled bike from the street. It looked like some big crushed insect.

"Which dry cleaner?"

"Caesar's on Clement Avenue at Third. Family's been there—forever."

At the place on the corner by the dry cleaner, Reba rang the bell several times, knocked on the door glass and finally handed her cake to a distraught young woman rushing in from a taxi who thanked her mutely with a nod. "For the family," Reba said.

When Reba got back home her apartment was too warm; she'd forgotten to turn off the oven. She did now, shuffled off her sodden poncho, and pulled the want ads from a trashcan under the sink. She slid her cell phone up from her dry pocket, put it on vibrate, laid it on the table, poured a class of milk, sat and spread out the want ads, and let the telephone, like an angry bee, buzz and buzz and buzz.

Burnt Sienna

The telephone rang in Veronica's Flower Shop. A woman calling said she'd be there in twenty minutes to return an orchid. Veronica parroted back, "Return an orchid?" No one had ever returned flowers before. "Is there a problem?" No answer. "Is it from this shop?" She knew it was. Veronica already knew that.

"Yeah. A gift," the girl said. "Will you be there? That hill is brutal."

"I live here," said Veronica.

The woman paused. "I'm coming," she said, and

hung up.

The one orchid delivery this week had been to an "R. Prentice." In fact, Veronica couldn't stop thinking of him. Of his beautiful hands accepting the papered pot from her at his front door. When a freak snowstorm had been forecast that day, Veronica closed shop early and made deliveries herself.

"How do we take care of it?" he asked.

"Well, it doesn't like cold," she replied, handing him the pot from within folds of her open pea coat.

"Come in," he entreated, his mellow voice and kind invitation sparking in Veronica an incongruous flash of desire.

Veronica stepped inside, rubbed her hands warm, and imparted details of light and water. All the time his gaze upon her bore a physical energy, until when their eyes met, Veronica slipped into the current of charged silence between them. Her throat caught, "Do you want to make sure it's OK?"

"Good idea." Resting the package on an entryway table, he reached into a drawer for scissors and with his beautiful hands used one blade to snap free the tape. The wrapping spiraled away and blossoms sprung free into an arc. "Lovely," he said, looking at Veronica.

Veronica lingered. "Orchids, more than any flower you could choose, embody love—and longing." She swallowed and touched the blossoms prattling on. "There's a story of the daughter of an ancient Mexican goddess who turned herself into an orchid so that she could be with her mortal lover, which was forbidden."

R. Prentice looked long at the orchid then, not at her, and said, his face red, "It's a gift."

"Oh," she said.

He reached close in front of her to re-open the door and stood in the doorway as Veronica backed toward her van buttoning up and leaving tracks in a fresh snowfall. "If you have any problem, call. Or stop by. I live at my shop. On the card..." She turned to the van to open the door, then called back… "Is the address."

R. Prentice lifted his chin in reply all the time watching her through whirling snowflakes.

She wondered if she would ever see him again. As Veronica mused about their brief encounter, she snipped the stems of unsold roses. Business at the shop had slowed now after the holidays. Also, there had been an accident on the hill, a stone wall broken, and one driving lane remained coned off. The caller was right; it was a treacherous road in winter. "Brutal," the caller said.

When she saw a car turning into the shop parking lot, Veronica laid the roses on the counter for the time being, washed her hands under the spigot and dried them. Soon the shop door jingled and a young woman entered, carrying the orchid unprotected in her gloved hands. "I want to return this." She pushed the pot at Veronica. "I don't have luck with them, I guess," she said, as she brushed loose soil from her coat sleeves.

Trembling as if *she* were the one who had come in from the cold, Veronica situated the orchid onto a lighted shelf. "Shop policy is no refunds. Do you want an exchange?"

"An exchange—that's funny." The woman stiffened. "No exchange."

Veronica studied this hybrid orchid's cascade of ivory blossoms, the heart of each one blushed green and painted with a set of burnt sienna-colored lines, like a bouquet of empty musical staffs awaiting notes to a love song. "In the right environment, orchids thrive."

"OK," the woman said. "I just don't want it." She swirled around to leave, stopped, and turned back. She took several steps toward Veronica. "I'm stuck with this image. My fiancé touching the orchid. Admiring it, I thought. Then he said… 'I have to see somebody.'"

Veronica caught her breath.

The woman watched Veronica's face. "He left—on a horrible night—and his car slid on ice."

"Is he…"

"He'll live." The woman stalked toward the door, then turned one more time. "I thought you'd be prettier," she said and yanked open the shop door. She slammed it shut, and the bell jingled.

Veronica knelt to pick up two red roses jarred from the counter to the floor, held them together in her still trembling hands, touched them to her lips, breathed their blended perfume and for the first time let herself believe that she would find him again.

Miracle At Black Rock

"John. Listen." My mother's hand tapping my neck drips with a tickle of dishwater. Her stage whisper is unnecessary because it isn't like my cousins, uncle, father and brother, can't hear her even though they've morphed into glowing TV football watching zombies.

"Five minutes, Mom."

"This will only take five minutes."

"Bills' defense is holding the opposing team at the five-yard line."

Football is white noise to my mother and not a

deterrent. She whispers, "When Leon comes out from the bathroom, please walk with him to his car. It's getting dark, the sidewalk's uneven. He'll break a hip. Here he comes..." Stage whisper. "... don't make me ask you in front of him."

"Jesus."

"Mind your mouth." She slaps more dishwater on me.

Leon, a snowy-haired retired gentleman, totters into the room and clears his throat. "Ahem...Bye all."

A chorus of "Bye, Leon." No heads turn, but hands are waved. The zombies do hear.

My Auntie Alfreda, sweaty faced and wearing a full body apron, rushes in from the kitchen like a gregarious wide receiver and pushes a huge container in which mashed potatoes and squash are major players into Leon's hands. "Here you go, Doll, you take care now."

I'm thinking—Great, Auntie Alfreda, throw off his balance. I get up; it's in my nature to be kind. My mother takes advantage.

"Leon, I'll carry that out for you," I say.

"Hey, you're watching the game."

"Hey, not right now," I lie. Behind Leon's back I give my mom stink eyes. She blows a kiss.

Outside, I one-arm the clunky potentially lethal container of leftovers and take Leon's arm to start down the slate steps thinking one loose piece or black ice could take us both out. I don't talk till the bottom so he can focus. Leon is one of Ma and Auntie Alfreda's Thanksgiving orphans, a retired police dispatcher who knows everybody--or, at least, he used to when he could remember them.

We reach the bottom. I ask him, "So you didn't want to see the end of the game, Leon?" We walk on down the sidewalk and watch for a chance to cross over to where he points to his parked car.

He stops walking when he talks. "I don't drive so good at night." He starts to walk again. Stops. Waves his hands in the air. "Besides, I want to be on the road before all the drunken crazies."

"Good thinking," I say, giving him a little starter nudge as we step off the curb to cross over. I don't talk again to keep him from stopping in the middle of the street. We reach his parked Chevy, a well-preserved relic of chrome and fins from Buffalo's glory Chevy days. Doing a kind of senior Macarena, Leon pats all the pockets in his coat and trousers and can't find his keys. I make small talk.

"Hey-- here's this year's Christmas tree." He stops looking for his keys. Mistake.

I point out a hefty balsam maybe twenty-five feet high behind the hedge in the yard of the closest house. Our breath launches little fog ghosts. I'm wishing I grabbed my coat, and I'm hugging the warm leftovers.

"You know that started out a reg'lar store bought Christmas tree?" Leon says.

"No kidding." I blow on my freezing fingers.

"Yup. The Dad joined the police force and stayed in the Army Reserves." His hand rubs his chin. "Must be thirty years ago he missed a Christmas and his wife had put the tree in the yard after Christmas and asked their kids to drag it to the curb to be collected." Leon stops to consider. "Must have been a warm winter."

"I wouldn't know what that's like...," I say shifting from one foot to the other, "...having grown up in the ice age."

"Heh. Heh. Well, instead of trashing the tree, the

daughter says she wants her dad to see it when he comes home. She wants to plant it. Kids." Leon shakes his head. "So the kids--Ruint a good snow shovel--dig a hole." He looks at me. "This is Black Rock. Digging a hole in this clay in this neighborhood in the wintertime in this city is a miracle all by and in itself. Anyhow..." Leon makes digging and patting motions. ".. they plant the tree, sawed off trunk and all." Leon stares at me. At first I thought he forgot what he was going to say. Then finally he says—in amazement, "And the damned thing takes root. It was sprouting out at the ends of the branches when I stopped by to see the Dad when he finally got back home the first Spring. It was him told me the story."

Silent, both of us breathe balsam breath and stare up at the extended arms of branches poised to catch the stars if they should fall.

"Thanks for that story, Leon," I say, and I mean it. On a hunch, I hunker down and look in through the car window. "Your keys are in the ignition."

"Oh, holy crap, is the door locked?"

I open it.

"OK, then." Leon folds himself into the car. "Happy Thanksgiving, Tom."

Tom's my lazy, less considerate brother, I want to say, but don't. "Happy Thanksgiving, Leon. Drive safe." The engine turns over pretty good, and he's off. I cup my hands, "Lights!" They come on.

I turn around, run back and take the slate steps three at a time. Wwruf, wwruf, wwruf. I think my jeans are freezing solid. When I get inside, I see the Bills have held them to a field goal and retaken the ball. "NEVER EVER say die." My voice cracks like ice. I jump around some to warm up, and backhand my mom the leftovers Leon and I forgot.

JAMAICA

Compass

"We read from pleasant Bibles that are bound in blood and skin."
~ Leonard Cohen

Every afternoon in those days, Terence, a youth about sixteen, rode an exhaust belching bus from his fine private school in sea level Kingston to his home high up in the Blue Mountains. Each day as the bus rounded a turn toward the apex of its afternoon run to Strawberry Hill, Terence would push open the middle door and jump off. Terence told me that he had asked the bus driver to make a special stop directly on the Gordon Town Road, but the driver wouldn't or couldn't stop because then all forward momentum to carry the laden bus up the mountain road would be lost. So, Terence, his forearms wrapped in his sweatshirt, punched open the middle door, jumped clear, and then bowed as passengers laughed and clapped. Daily passengers anticipated the entertainment. The bus driver "made a meal" of scolding him, Terence said, but took to leaving loose the door. Most days Terence jumped off because he loved being dramatic, on other days, though, he had his own special reason to hurry into Gordon Town.

A lot of people were in a hurry, a hurry to leave the country. The media was full of two news items: the tragic illness afflicting the great singer/songwriter Bob Marley, and the coming election. Air Jamaica advertised "five flights a day to Miami" that summer of 1980. Neighbor Fidel Castro's mentoring stirred up as much fear of loss in people as hope of gain, so there were many goodbyes from the richer to the poorer. When I left the island, I did not do a good job of saying good-bye to Terence. His memory chafes as if etched on internal beach glass lodged in my heart.

Terence had an immediate practical reason to hurry twice a week, because, besides suffering the weight of a backpack full of schoolbooks, he hefted a cotton flour sack full of groceries, which he would trade for piano lessons at Miss Mae's in Gordon Town. Terence had literally to beat the heat by walking at top speed or jogging up the remaining one half mile to Gordon Town because Miss Mae often ordered a pint of vanilla ice cream and a quarter pound of butter. Goods were rationed in Kingston in the shadow of possible impending Communism, and "luxuries" were impossible to find up in Gordon Town.

Miss Mae, my landlady, owned three cottages on her riverside property: one she lived in, two she rented out—one to me, an expatriate teacher from Philadelphia—and one to a Jamaican policeman, his wife and two children.

Miss Mae was a strict music teacher. Before she would let Terence touch the piano, he had to beat out the rhythm of the day's piece with drumsticks on a board. After attending for a long hour to Miss Mae's unrelenting demands for exact rhythms, proper hand position, and allegiance to the rigors of producing beautiful classical music that was more Western than West Indian in its composition, Terence would stop by my tiny cottage for comic relief. Our friendship's tradition was that I'd mix two tall, Morir de Sueños, a drink made of iced fresh orange juice and condensed milk, which Terence and I called the Marilyn Monroe of milks because of its voluptuous consistency. "Morir de Sueños" means to die dreaming.

Sometimes Terence helped me wash and fill glass jars to make yogurt. Or some days, with the neighbor policeman's children, a boy and girl, we'd fold newspaper boats to race on the river, or craft hand puppets with coconut shells for heads to have a show. We acted out the Anansi stories they all knew. Terence preferred to be Tiger, but his crackling adolescent voice and wise guy nature fit the sly spider, and we would beg him to be Anansi. We taped the dialogs on a cassette tape recorder for my children's literature students at St. Joseph's College in Kingston.

One day the four of us while playing around the river, had gotten our feet slick with mud. The policeman's children said if they went home "dutty so," their mother would fret. On my back porch high above the mud of the river, while sitting cross-legged around a large cast aluminum pot of warm soapy water, we made a game of washing our feet. I washed my own foot with a soft washrag of terrycloth, rinsed and wrung out the cloth, and washed one of the feet of the policeman's small boy next to me. He in turn rinsed the sudsy rag and washed his other foot and one foot of Terence's and Terence one of his own and one of the little girl's and she one of mine and I her other one. There was a completeness and fraternity in this friendship ceremony.

When the policeman's children were busy elsewhere, Terence and I would talk. We called it "chatterboxing." We'd "chatterbox" or play dominoes sometimes till "first stars" when Terence had to go home to finish homework. On this next day, I was leaving, going back to the States, garnering a cache of golden memories of my stay in the tropics and moving on to a new life. I didn't mean to hurt anybody, but where people are there's really no escape from sin.

On this penultimate day of my stay on the island, I tapped out on my antique Smith Corona typewriter- which I promised to Miss Mae- the final Children's Literature exam grades to mail in to the college from the airport. The click click of the typewriter was suddenly drowned out by a Clackity Clackity Snap POW as Terence played his hand-carved mahoe drumsticks over the spine of the stiff, vertical wooden jalousies in my front window. Terence stood long and lean; his skin honey golden. His eyes, almond-shaped and brown as burnt sugar glowed with warm fire he could also share in a wide smile of beautiful white teeth, blessed in their whiteness by the honey brown of his skin, and the true black of his hair. Miss Mae said Terence "lit up her day." She didn't say this to Terence, because he was "brash enough," but she confided in me that she took great pride in his talent and potential.

"Music is my ticket," Terence would say. His hands danced with drumsticks the way a dandy swings with panache an inlaid walking stick; the way cowboys draw and pack pearl-handled revolvers. He holstered his drumsticks under his belt sheathed in the pants pocket of his beige school uniform. Whenever inspired by primal energy charging his body and soul, he'd retrieve them and tap rhythms he gleaned from the moment to translate to the rest of us what set his nerves to sing.

Home for Terence was a tin-roofed cinder-block house on the fringe of Gordon Town set on a winding mountain road that ran like a sinewy handle along the Gordon River toward Kingston, which lay uneasily simmering in its broad valley frying pan. When one looked up at Gordon Town at night from the hot city, streetlights formed a constellation against the dark mountains' silhouette. Terence's house was under the southernmost "star."

Terence used no last name. The country people

referred to his mother as a crazy white Jamaican "mule," a mule being a woman who cannot bear children. That she had a son did not change their opinion. She would have to have three children to raise her status, and she would have to care. The boy's mother kept to herself. Perhaps she was shy, although she had not infected Terence with any lack of self-esteem. To make a scant living she took in sewing and laundering, and did some cooking for a Catholic church in a town higher up the mountains. Once a week, Father Chong Lee, a Chinese Jamaican priest who drove a beat-up red pick-up would drop off and retrieve laundered, mended and embroidered vestments and collect baked goods.

Terence ventured on his own to ask Miss Mae to be his piano teacher. Miss Mae had played the accompaniment for ballet dancers as a profession before she retired. Terence introduced himself to me when he discovered me in the cottage at Miss Mae's. He was amused by my sign over the door— "Cubicle Sweet Cubicle."

"Miss Pamela come now," Terence called in to me as I typed the final grades. "My lesson finish. Your lesson should a finish."

Like Miss Mae, I looked forward to Terence's visits.

While Terence sang and beat time to timeless reggae songs, which drifted across the rushing Gordon River from the jukebox at the El Paso Cafe on Gordon Town's main street, I squeezed fresh orange juice and presented two iced Morir de Sueños. The happy marriage of milk and orange juice was refreshing, even nutritious.

"You ready to marry me yet?" Terence's long, brown fingers brushed away a milk mustache, then one-handed he twirled a chair into place at the long, low table on my porch, his drumsticks holstered on his hip at the ready.

"I'm not going to be anybody's ticket to the U.S., Terence. It's illegal, it's not the right thing to do, and teachers don't marry students."

"Music is my ticket," he said too softly and his eyes looked someplace far away. "When exactly are you leaving us?"

I lifted a blue glass bottle of red hibiscus that were beginning to coil closed for the evening to the table's center. "The newspapers are calling Kingston a mini-Beirut. We heard gunshots at the college Monday. It's a free election, but people are fearful and want to influence the outcome. I'm going back to the U.S. tomorrow. Until the election is over, and things settle down." It was a litany I'd recited often.

He'd started when I said tomorrow, but Terence was his cool self when he said, "You're not coming back. Not for some time. Never to live here again."

"I knew everything at sixteen, too." I scolded, "You're a baby."

"Enough lecturin. You don get pay for dat here ooman. I brought you a present, Darlin," he said. He pulled a rolled up piece of parchment that he must have gotten from school on which was drawn a compass rose in a clear, distinct hand. "This is so you can find out where is right and wrong, because findin out right and wrong is what you so like to do."

He'd sketched no country, only the compass rose.

"How am I supposed to know where is right and wrong?"

"Me no know, truly, but I would suppose that right is towards the heat of the sun and back to us." He swallowed, "back to me."

I blushed and turned away. "Thank you. I wish I thought it was that easy."

"You think too much. Say, are you going to sell your tape recorder? I need one to tape my music."

"No, I need my tape recorder for my job." So many times since I've mentally deleted that sentence and offered up the gift he desired savoring the gratitude in his eyes. But in reality I said, "I have a present for you, too."

I took a pair of Blue Willow salt and peppershakers from my cupboard. It was too damp to use the saltshaker by the river, so I never used them. "Here is right." I handed him the saltshaker. "... And wrong." I handed him the pepper. "Do right, Terence, and walk good." I made a living of lecturing.

"I'll really miss you." He said it nasal to poke fun at an American accent. Then clearly he said, "Marry me instead."

"It wouldn't be right," I said too quickly, avoiding his eyes.

"Ah, salt doan marry pepper, eh? I'll give these to my mother."

The rest of the evening Terence helped me pack. I gave him incidentals to take home in a pillow case, things I couldn't fit into my bulging suitcase.

At "first stars" he rose to go. I hugged him, but couldn't say good-bye. His eyes were uncharacteristically tragic. "I'll stop by the bus stop in Gordon Town in the morning and say good-bye." I felt him tug at my fingertips as we swept apart forever.

After Terence left, I went to the Policeman's house to have some cake with the family and say good-bye to the children, returning to my dark, empty cottage about 10 O'clock; the moon was high in the sky. To fill the silence, I decided to tape some souvenir bits on Miss Mae's radio. Then I realized my tape recorder was missing.

My face flushed with anger, I marched out into the night past the already darkened policeman's house. I didn't think about any danger of being out alone at night until in the middle of the bridge into town I narrowly escaped being hit by an overloaded livestock truck making a late run into Kingston. Brakes squealed. The driver swore at me, and then hooted did I want a ride when he saw I was a young woman alone. I ignored him.

When I reached Terence's, I stepped off the public road into the dark, Jasmine and food-scented privacy of his mother's house. My own sense of violation made it too easy for me to violate their territory. Even in my anger, I didn't want to give him away to his mother. I moved around to the back of the house and hoarsely whispered,

"Terence, I want it back. Give it to me now," I threatened. "I'll come in and get it if I have to."

The catch on the back door rattled and Terence's slim, brown body emerged. He wore bed clothes, only dark colored shorts. Silently he handed me a pillowcase with what I knew was the tape recorder inside. Our skin didn't touch. We didn't speak. We didn't look into each other's eyes. We were cold strangers. There would be no more gifts. I started wearily back up the hill to my empty house.

I'd moved to the left side of the road so I could watch out for any traffic. My self-righteous anger and grief blinded me and, even though its headlights were shining, I was almost upon the livestock truck that had backed up and pulled to my side of the road before I considered it a threat. Assuming the driver was in the cab, I hurried past. The squeals and grunts of pigs riding to their slaughter came from behind a canvas cover. For an instant, I envied their imperviousness to emotional pain, then I laughed out loud at my presumption and the absurdity of my envy. A dark man pretending to smooth the canvas covering appeared too quickly from the back of the truck.

"You laugh?" he said with a foolish almost hopeful grin. I started to the right. He wheeled right, too, and moved closer. I swung at him with the pillowcase to fend him off. "You carry a pillow for us, ow sweet." He caught the end of the pillowcase and made to wrap it around me. He sweat alcohol. I turned around, too, to stay free of him.

"No. NO." I yelled. "Leave me alone," my voice feeble with fear.

Suddenly a white woman burst out from Terence's house. She must have been watching me take my leave. Her long straight hair was loose and flying about in a glorious mane in the light of the headlights. She wore a long cotton nightgown and had untied athletic sneakers on her feet. In her raised arms she wielded a glinting machete. I saw her first. When she reached the truck, she spun her "sword" in a low round swing like an Arab and made to slash at the tires. The driver followed my eyes, released me in a panic and swore. "Rass Clot. woman yo mad." He muscled me aside, fumbled at the handle of the door of his truck, scrambled in, released the brake to start his escape, got the ignition going and chugged off.

My savior stalked him for a few steps, shaking the machete above her head. "Good riddance. Your pigs are more human." While the truck moved away, she jumped, shaking the machete and screamed, "Ya rattid."

She turned then to me. "Do you care to come back and spend the night?"

I thought of Terence and of leaving in the morning. "No," adrenaline both fueled my words and weighed them down. "My neighbor is a policeman. He has a gun."

"Go on, then, I'll watch till you reach the bridge. If you call out after that, I'll hear you."

I thanked her and walked and ran home on legs of water. I went inside, locked the door behind me, dragged a chair in front of it, and lay awake on the bed most of my last night on the island.

In the morning, milky mist still rolled on the river when the driver I hired arrived to take me to the airport. To save petrol he coasted the car packed and heavy with my trunks and bags down the hill. A crowd of boys in khaki uniforms jostled at the bus stop in Gordon Town. I spotted Terence, but his back was turned. I watched to see if he would turn around, but I let distance pull me away with no word to the driver. My mind was on the salt and peppershakers I found at my door, which rattled now like dry bones where I threw them into my suitcase next to the tape recorder.

On the plane, the engines' drone made me feel as if I was being vacuumed off the island. At baggage claim in Miami, I opened my suitcase to get a raincoat and found bits of broken china mixed with salt and pepper. I scattered the mess like ashes in a lounge trash container. I longed to send the tape recorder back to Terence immediately, but now it was dirty, and, anyway, he wouldn't be able to afford the duty tax.

When I found a job, I sent money for Terence to buy a tape recorder at the inflated price on the island economy. I included a money order in a noisy letter about how sorry I was and how I should have given him the tape recorder in the first place. The envelope came back unopened and marked "deceased." For the first time, I felt the broken glass twist inside me.

My fingers trembled as I dialed Miss Mae's telephone number.

"Robson residence, Mae Robson speaking." Miss Mae answered in genteel English. When appropriate, she would slip into patois.

"Miss Robson, this is Pam Pasmore," I heard myself say. "I need to find out about Terence."

"Oh. Yes, dear. Pamela. Hello. It's terrible. Terrible."

"Then he's really gone."

"It was a terrible mistake."

I thought of my mistake.

Miss Mae's voice was tired. "Of a Friday last month I had only just collected the post in town and was coming back over the bridge when the tenant children ran up to me. The little girl grasped on so to me. 'Miss Mae, Terence is shot.' 'Dead.' the boy said. 'Dead and Daddy carry him back like Jesus.' I looked up and saw their father carrying Terence in his arms. A crowd followed with one of the men out ahead to clear traffic. They carried him down so to his mother's. I'm told some kind soul drove up the ridge to bring back Father Chong Lee."

"What happened? Why, Terence?" My throat gripped at my words.

"It was a terrible mistake. A tragic mistake." Miss Mae continued, "With the election coming on there's been a number of disturbances. Extra police are called up from Kingston. They don't know the people over here. This day a mob up at Mavis Bank hooted and sang and clapped about the new day coming. Terence, they say, swung out his drumsticks quick, quick, and a town policeman shot him as the man took it for the drawing of a weapon." Terence stood out in a crowd, a trait disadvantageous in a riot.

"How's his mother?" My throat squeezed.

"Gone. She's gone. Terence is buried in the churchyard by Father Chong Lee's…"

A twist of the shard of glass.

"… And Father has already moved in a young family from Trenchtown to take over Terence house. I don't know where is his mother. She isn't at the house again."

I thanked Miss Mae, gave her my mailing address, and made an empty promise to visit.

I mourned Terence. I gave the tape recorder to a startled young black boy who had his smile. Within the year, I received a letter:

"Dear Miss Pasmore,

Miss Mae Robson gave me your address. I know that Terence enjoyed being friends with you. I was glad because you were an American and I thought that when he was 18, and we came to the States together, he could look you up and maybe you could help him get started in a job or something. You know that Terence is my son, what you may not have realized, is that I am an American. I lived in Jamaica as an expatriate as you did.

I had been in Jamaica for two years when I found out I was pregnant. My parents in the states would not accept a racially mixed child. My father sent me money to 'come home alone.' If I wouldn't consent to an abortion, my parents wanted me to give Terence up for adoption. Neither was an option for me. I wasn't married to Terence's father, but he paid my hospital bill and signed the birth certificate. In Jamaica, men have all rights to their children. I *couldn't leave the country legally with Terence, and I wouldn't leave without him. When my parents became resigned to our situation, they sent money off and on, and I was able to send Terence to a good private school. With the help of Father Chong Lee, I kept my papers in order, and laid low in Gordon Town pretending to be a white Jamaican, so I could wait things out until Terence turned 18. I never told Terence I wasn't a born Jamaican. At 18, he could claim his U.S. citizenship and leave on his own. We almost made it. I wanted you to know that he valued your friendship and was ashamed because..."*

I stopped reading. This woman, Helen Scrimshaw of Marietta, Georgia, gave Terence his life, and spent her years caring for him in a foreign country. Terence gave me beautiful memories of a fine friendship. I didn't even give him a gift he sorely wanted. I didn't even say good-bye.

While I was searching for tapes of the Anansi stories to send his mother, I remembered with another twist of the glass inside me the compass rose that Terence had drawn. I took it out of my Bible where I'd pressed it flat among the pages of Isaiah—the prophet poet. On the back I wrote:

"Dear Terence,

Your music and beauty were your ticket to our hearts. You died dreaming.

That's a haunting way to say good-bye."

I sent the tapes and the framed compass rose to his mother that same day because the vitality of a generous act is as fleeting as butter in the sun, the vibrations of tapping drumsticks, a heart beating, and the opportunity to tell somebody's story.

Designated Smoking Area

[Handwritten annotation: Character's name changed to Lennart to distinguish from Claude McKay in next story.]

Tonight, a stationery red light burned over the exit door on the hospital's loading platform. Above that a full moon, puller of tides and governor of vast arrivals and departures, shone among glistening stars. ~~Claude~~ *Lennart* Blackstone had a poignant memory of the stars following him to the United States and of shrinking.

As a little child, Claude and his family had been swept to the United States on a tide of immigrants who feared that their island motherland, Jamaica, after an impending election would follow Cuba into Communism.

Claude didn't so much fear Communism then, which he didn't understand, as much as he longed for security in the midst of change. He had only a child's grasp of impending events. After his father revealed their Florida destination, Claude told friends that the family was moving to "my Daddy's Ammy."

The only familiar comfort in his new world was the stars. The stars had been bigger in Jamaica, closer. Or maybe his family grew smaller on the journey. That must be it because sometimes it seemed as if they had grown so small in this new fussy glitzy city that they were invisible. Claude spent his life in America trying to be larger, to be seen again. At that time, in accordance with his magical childhood logic, the stars, the same stars he remembered from Jamaica, always appeared in the darkest, most scary hours, and had power to protect him. Looking to them for solace became a lifelong inclination.

Even when he became a grown-up soldier medic in Kandahar, Afghanistan, he looked to those same stars to temper the chaos of war with some order and sanity. Claude's time in the Army secured his U.S. citizenship, and as soon as he could, Claude left the Army, started college classes, and took this civilian job as a nurse's aide. He could only get hired on the late-night shift.

Tonight, Claude had finished helping a patient with a catheter and bed pan, then in weariness collapsed onto the room's one chair. The patient, an elderly gentleman, kindly turned out the light. Claude slept and dreamed that he was being mistaken for an enemy soldier, pushed face down and lying in the mud, his wrists and ankles tightly bound. He woke with a start, relieved that the ropes and restraints were all in his head, the ghosts of too many administrative intrusions. A nurse's aide had nothing but bosses. Claude looked over to see that the patient slept soundly. He needed a break outside in the fresh air under the stars.

Claude burst onto the loading platform to vent and to smoke, to cure himself of his current frustration. On this graveyard shift, he didn't expect any company. He grabbed onto the rail and roared, "ARGHH—H—H—GRH," then pounded it with both hands. "Rahtid—petty—regulations. When's my vote?"

He'd come a long way. His hard work and mastery of technical skills were beginning to be noticed, respected, taken seriously, trusted, but this notice and respect stopped short of Claude's leonine ambition. With a tap, he reminded himself to take a needed physical break. He sat on the top rail to take the weight off, hooked aching feet onto the lower rail, and with an undulating wave of his fingers invited fresh air and the starry sky to celebrate the release of his latex glove-muffled hands.

As he balanced on the platform rail, Claude grinned remembering another starlit October night when he was stationed in Hawaii. His active duty girlfriend, Sharonna, begged to sleep on the beach. At sunset, they lay in the mist of crescendoing emerald waves at Ehukai Beach on Oahu's north shore. The blanketed sand was with the darkness cold, so Claude, as his father used to do on Jamaica's beaches, gathered bush for kindling, kicked, wrested free and dragged a driftwood log from where it clung to a high bank and assembled a bonfire. Soon threads of embers soared up to join the stars and Claude and Sharonna, enraptured and alone, joined bodies. Building bonfires was illegal, but sometimes you must take chances to enjoy life.

"Yasso sweet," Claude whispered aloud. From his chest pocket, he drew matches and a cigarette, positioned it between his lips, and struck a match. His cigarette breathed a sole lambent ember.

A tiny piccolo voice floated up out of the darkness, "You shouldn't smoke cigarettes."

What the hell? Near the steps that descended to the parking lot Claude could just make out a kid in what appeared to be a butterfly costume sitting wings against the wall near a heating vent, her black leotarded legs crossed at the ankle, glittery antennae on her headband bobbling, eyes hidden by a black half mask. She had positioned open on her lap a pillowcase full of candy and was tearing open a Snickers. He may have woken her up.

"Your parents know where you are so late, Missy?"

She didn't reply.

"Where're your parents?" Claude repeated. He wondered about how to handle this without upsetting the child.

"I'm not allowed to talk to strangers. Anyway, my dad's gone with the Army."

"Does your mother know where you are?"

"She will. She's really smart."

"You live in base housing?"

She chewed and swallowed a huge bite of candy bar. "Yesh."

"OK then."

Claude looked up the base number on his smart phone. "OOD, please…Lieutenant, there's a little girl here at the hospital… No, the civilian hospital on Madison. That's right…No, no! Not hurt. Wandered over, I guess. She's eating Halloween candy…Yeah, I figured. Tell Mom beyond the ER is a Designated Smoking Area. We'll be right there… My name is Claude Blackstone… I work here. Nurse Assistant. I'm on break, but I'll stay with her till her mother comes…Yes, my cell phone. Bye Lieutenant… Prior. Yes. Thank you."

Claude sat down on the top step some distance from the child. "How'd you get all the way over here from base?"

"Tricker Treating. My new sister got sick, so my mom couldn't take me. I got upset. She said all right then I could go with some kids, but not to cross our street." She had finished with the Snickers and rooted through her bag for another treat. Before opening another selected chocolate bar, she drew out a long pack of rainbow-colored gum balls and offered them to Claude. "Would you like these? I don't."

"No thank you," Claude said. "You crossed the street, didn't you?"

"The kids did, too. Then they went into their house and said I should go home."

"Why'd you come here?"

"I didn't know how to go home, but I saw the hospital, and anyway I was born here."

"Your mother had you at this hospital?"

"My birth mother."

Claude was silent.

"My mom and dad wanted a baby, and they couldn't have one then, but they found me here."

"They adopted you."

"Yes. After my mom brought home my sister from the Army hospital, she showed me this hospital and said my birth mother had me here, where my mom and dad found me… to adopt."

"You're a lucky girl," Claude said.

"Yes."

A blue-lighted military police car entered the parking lot and stopped. A young woman rushed out first, ran over and scooped the butterfly child from the step into her arms. "Clemmie, thank God." Claude picked up the pillowcase and handed it to the MP following close behind who reached out for it. They nodded to each other eye to eye. The young mother stuttered to Claude in confusion, "Thank you SO MUCH. I didn't know she would go so far. I don't know how she got over here."

"She told me the older kids left her. Anyway, no problem, Ma'am. How's the baby?"

"She's OK…with my neighbor."

"That's good. Night, Clementine," Claude said, his own vexation disarmed by this faithful disoriented little pilgrim. "Listen to your Mama now and be safe."

The butterfly lifted the chin buried in her mother's shoulder. "Bye. Anyway, how'd you know my name?"

"I'm really smart," Claude said.

Riding the Train with Claude McKay

ChiChi boarded the commuter train at JFK in Jamaica, New York, vastly different than the Jamaica, West Indies she flew out of this morning. The train car quickly filled with scuttling passengers, all strangers, securing bags and finding seats. All these people foreigners to her. ChiChi felt akin only to the train window holograph looking back at her scared and tired. Too soon she'd disembark in Manhattan to fashion her new life.

Poison dart doubts agitated her whenever she thought about being so "by herself." Her palms sweat.

She felt her heart thrump within her chest. To calm down, she thumbed open Mama's parting gift to her, the Claude McKay poetry book Mama engraved "Remember your roots." Two poems on the page, "Home Thoughts" about a boy climbing for mangoes, and "Broadway" about a "hundred shouting signs" only served to stretch ChiChi between two cultures. She closed her eyes. The steady rhythm of the train lulled her from a rack of anxiety into sleep and the broad sling of a dream.

Train sounds dissolved and into her sleeping consciousness drifted a kind-eyed, red-capped porter in an old-fashioned uniform. He adjusted the jacket rolled up behind her head just as Papa would fluff her pillow after finding her asleep over homework.

"Mind you rest, Missy," he crooned in familiar Jamaican cadence.

"Ticket's been punched," ChiChi slurred.

"No problems," he said and then sat down.

He wept, his face glistening ebony. "I left my Mama to travel to New York, too. Our mothers don't want to, but they throw us into their dreams and say 'You fly away.' They say, 'I did not go so far a foreign. You must take this opportunity to bless America with your holy self.'"

ChiChi moaned. "Why'd I ever leave home?"

"One leaves eventually by chance or choice," the Porter said. "You and I chose a dazzling place." He made a stern face. "It'll shake you." He pressed his knuckles hard together. "But if you stand up against each pack of dogged challenges, you'll find the magic of a space to say 'I burn deep. My fire heals.' "

"Auntie Justine Nethersole acted on the stage in Manhattan," ChiChi said, "but she slipped and broke her heart and moved back with us." Excavating confidence, ChiChi imitated Auntie's grand voice, "Dress modest, Daughter. Reign proud. Shun any wolfish Mr. Mention." ChiChi eyed the Porter, "Who are you?"

He tapped ChiChi's book of poems, "I stirred raw Jamaican honey into Harlem grit and bitterness."

"You're the poet Claude McKay who worked on the railroad long ago."

"Do you know your name?" he asked.

"I'm called ChiChi. Like birds' songs."

"Birdsong and flower breath," he mused. "Memories of sweet Jamaica sustained me. My poems will sustain you when sometimes New York City overwhelms in terms of unfamiliar rush and crowd. Girl, neither King Street Market nor Crossroads at dusk generates such a big confusion."

"Yes, Sir," ChiChi said. "My brother TomTee must drive across Kingston town day in, day out in his old rundown taxi. 'Watch right and left in the city,' he says, 'or one metro bus running hell and powder house down the avenue will mash you up.'"

The Porter nodded, "Even on sidewalks crushes of people--from every land--comprise an ocean of eyes, elbows and lumbering feet. Move along or move across to the store windows." His brown eyes shone. "Missy, at Christmastime see there our wild flame-heart poinsettias transplanted into pots. See in those windows joyous stories."

He rubbed his hands together and a decorated Christmas tree appeared with Mama and Papa sitting thigh to thigh on a sofa admiring it. Underneath, new eyeglasses for myopic Auntie Nethersole stuck out of a long skinny stocking. Parked incongruously nearby appeared a sunburst-yellow taxicab. A gift tag taped to the windshield read "For TomTee from ChiChi. Paid in full."

The Porter continued, "Snow inside the windows shines a-glitter fine enough, but if real snow falls…Ah-h-h, Missy, then feathers of lacy ice twirl slowly down and settle as fleeting jewels on the dark of your forearm."

He clapped hands like Mama does to demand attention, "At your new school you will be hungry. Eat food at every opportunity."

Eat food. Her grumbling stomach woke her. And the slowing rhythm and screech of the train laboring into Penn Station. ChiChi awoke anticipating wonders. In haste, she stood and the book slid to the floor. The man beside her picked it up and handed it back.

"I won't forget you," said ChiChi turning to the puzzled ordinary passenger. "I mean, Thank you." The train pitched to a complete stop and ChiChi took her place in the line of diligent passengers nudging at straps and shifting loads preparing like paratroopers to leap into The Melting Pot.

HAWAII

SITE-FAITHFUL

*"They're so strongly site-faithful
[thePacific Golden Plover, Kolea in Hawaiian]
that we can predict where they will be with almost
100% accuracy."*

~ PlanetEarth Online

On my first flight south to the island, Johnny's yard attracted me like a square-cut emerald. Others in my flock chose the vast green of rolling golf courses and institutional grounds for their fall and winter turf, but Johnny's tidy place suited me. After a day or two of dodging, I discovered a small Post Office across the street from Johnny's yard where I could perch on the red tile roof for a clear view of the thrashing sea while Johnny mowed the lawn with his hand mower or his wife hung laundry.

Johnny built this house, was still building it, a solid two-bedroom starter home with walls of concrete block that termites would break their jaws on, a dream house for his wife complete with room for a garden (my particular comfort), a pretty hand-hewn Dutch door and a white picket fence to protect children maybe, but there were no children. No children and no hissing cats made life amenable for me, but all of this, the lush island, the sturdy house, and the tended garden did not satisfy Johnny's wife's appetites. During that first late fall and winter while Johnny was away at work I noticed the presence of another man.

And while sunning on the roof at the Post Office, I heard Bixby, the meddlesome Post Master, tell postal workers, he even talked story to local customers at the pay window, that Johnny's wife's guest with whom she was "having an affair, of course" was a teacher from the University where she sometimes worked. Unsuspecting, Johnny continued to labor about his house and garden every weekend as I waited on the roof of the Post Office for the first opportunity to flit into a quiet yard, which I admit I had begun thinking of as my own.

In March, my colors transmuted from a breast of speckled brown wood-tone to black obsidian, and when I acquired the soldierly band of snowy white across my forehead and neck, Johnny and his wife still lived together in the little house. More and more often, though, Johnny's wife went missing on weekends when Johnny mowed the lawn. Also, she took to hanging the clothes on a weekday morning and leaving them uncollected rain or shine. That same day she would leave in a car with the man before lunch and return with no groceries before dinner and before Johnny got home. I admit I enjoyed walking under drying laundry that rode in the breeze like many colored flags and cast dancing shadows on the luscious insect rich lawn. I left the island one April morning on her clothes hanging day so I could carry the image of the colored flags and dancing shadows in my head while I braved the long, lonely, gray ocean on my migration.

In August I returned, a mature brown-speckled bird with flecks of gold on my back, having bred and fostered a family with my mate on Alaska's unrelenting tundra.

Site-Faithful

Chilled breezes and my wandering wing prompted me to fly back to the toasty islands and back to Johnny's yard, my garden gem. Over the next few weeks, I didn't see Johnny's wife even one time. I noticed, as well, the hanging laundry robbed of quantity and color, the yard on early mornings, weekends, and evenings hectic and noisy with hammer blows and sanding whirs because Johnny was building a large boat. More and more I sat upon the Post Office roof or flitted about town hoping for the renewed peace of my beloved emerald garden.

Bixby the Postmaster gossiped about Johnny's sudden habit "he's a boozer and a loser" that had cost him his job and most likely his sanity. Johnny worked on this boat all day every day into the evening. He carried on about using the boat to fetch his wife who had abruptly left for the mainland with the university professor.. The idea of building the boat to bring her back came to Johnny in a dream he said; this idea Bixby mocked with his brand of noxious glee. Bixby touted that the dreamcatcher tattoo on Johnny's upper arm branded him "a loony bird from the get go" with too much faith in dreams.

What made Bixby meddlesome about Johnny's boat

was the carrion of scandal and the opportunity to gossip. Bixby, at any opportunity, pulled up a lawn chair right outside Johnny's fence. Each workday, at lunch break, Bixby slipped out of his sandals, rolled up his blue uniform pant legs to sun his chubby white legs, unwrapped his lunch, a sandwich and a drink in a thermos, and hovered like a fat fly. "Holy Christmas, what a nut case. Wire you building a boat?" He trilled at Johnny with that question day after day. "Wire you building a boat? Wire you building a boat?"

In the morning, when Bixby first arrived at work, Johnny's voice answered husky and intent, "To bring back my wife." Bixby would shake his head then and, without a comforting word, turn the key to the Post Office door.

"Wire you building a boat? Wire you building a boat?" Bixby's goading went on and on at midday, as irritating as a jaybird. By lunchtime, Johnny slurred, "Goin to fesh my wife. Thash the plan. To bring her back."

"Holy Christmas," Bixby bantered with a mouthful of sandwich. "Your wife is in Podunk for Chrissake. I know. I forward her mail. Give it up nutcase."

"I'm feshing my-y-y wi-i-ife." His broken voice as searing as a lark's cry, Johnny swung around one time and nearly fell from the hull of the boat.

Bixby grinned, "Rough seas today, nutcase," and pulled at his sandwich like a common street pigeon.

Peering through her window in the "Ono Plate Lunch" food wagon parked next to the Post Office, Kahiau saw Johnny wheel about and almost fall; I saw her wince. Her name, I heard say, means in Hawaiian: one who gives asking nothing in return. Many days hour after hour I saw Kahiau admire Johnny's diligent lean body, tanned amber, clenched in a beneficial masculine dance in utter contrast to Bixby's doughy smugness. A flutter of my wings saluted her ardor.

Johnny had come by the food wagon a few times when his wife was still with him. The wagon sat close enough to the house that Kahiau, like me, could hear them arguing about the wife being too tired to deal with dinner. Johnny would always come, not the wife. "Two chicken plates."

"Anything to drink?"

"No. Thanks."

Johnny didn't really see Kahiau. He didn't note, like I did, the catch in her throat at his closeness. She was a young working girl to him, not a grown woman with feelings for him.

The first couple of times Kahiau passed by in the evening stealing glances of Johnny and Johnny's boat on her walk home she did nothing when she saw him passed out cold, but I could sense that she longed to nurture him. Kahiau favors my kind of mate; her giving spirit is admirable across species. One evening Bixby had left the Post Office at least an hour before Kahiau called it a day at the food wagon. Johnny thrashed in drunken unconsciousness. Kahiau looked around and saw no one, but I saw her. I saw Kahiau lift her flowered skirt and climb into the boat shell where she gently pulled the bottle of rum from Johnny's hand and pushed in its place what looked to be a bottle of strong coffee. When her hand brushed his tattooed arm, Kahiau swooned like a swan. Replacing rum with bracing coffee became a daily ritual.

On the strength of her awakened fervid sensations, Kahiau gained courage. One day I cried out excited and pleased when Kahiau jangled the Dutch door, found it unlocked and entered to leave a plate of meat and rice in Johnny's fridge.

Driven, Johnny continued his feverish boat building mission using alcohol to fend off loneliness. But he wasn't alone, I saw Kahiau pay many little attentions to Johnny. When there was a lull of customers at the food wagon, she carried him a jug of water and ice to refill a pitcher left next to the boat. Johnny nodded. His dream was to bring back his wife. Her quiet attention showed that Kahiau respected people's dreams, that she had dreams of her own.

Bixby, on the other hand, acted as if Johnny was crazy. Taunting Johnny at lunchtime became Bixby's recreation. "How's the dry-dock dingy dingy coming?" Bixby rolled up his pant legs, emptied his sandals of feet, crossed his fat legs at the ankles, unwrapped his sandwich and settled in for a daily dessert of taunts.

Daily Kahiau became more brazen. One evening, she stole Johnny's dirty laundry, carried it home to wash, and, the next evening, on her walk home from the food wagon, she returned clean clothes to Johnny's house. There's something to be said for being able to change clothes; my colors had begun to change again with approaching spring. During the next day when Kahiau watched him from her lunch wagon window, she smiled seeing that Johnny's white T-shirt, sweet and fresh, hugged his laboring tan arms and back as his love boat took shape.

I believe Kahiau knows something about boats. I often see Kahiau's father take her fishing on weekends. On their fishing boat, as she must have done from the time she was a child, she rides the bow. It is clear that she enjoys the chill of her wet clinched fingers as she clings to the bow like a carved figurehead when her father sweeps the boat out of the marina into the mist-ridden early morning sea. I did see Johnny look at her one day while he was down at the marina purchasing a boat motor. Kahiau, thighs hugging the boat, wind combing her raven hair up and away, Kahiau tasting the salt of the sea and sharing the soul of a great sea bird soaring over the surf. Kahiau, my sister, beautiful, brave and free.

More than any of her brothers and sisters, Kahiau spends whole days at sea while one of them tends the weekend business of the lunch wagon. Kahiau shares the labor of carrying her father's boat back to the water whenever it has been dry-docked for cleaning or repair. Like me, she knows the joy of leaving the stubborn gravity of dry land for the water's slick ease. After a day of rolling on the

Site-Faithful

sea, sunned and salted, she helps her father fill an old oil drum with fresh water gurgling like liquid silver from the garden hose. Kahiau's father attaches the small motor to a brace fashioned on the water-filled drum to let the motor run clear of corrosive salt water. Her father teaches her to care for things as well as people. Even we Koleas know: working tools, mechanical or alive in the form of a human or Kolea body, merit maintenance.

Directly behind where Johnny works on the boat is a cement storm drain about twelve feet wide. The day she started retrieving Johnny's laundry, Kahiau took to slipping down into the runoff drain to reach her parents' home; the distance is shorter, and she could enter her own room in the back, mix Johnny's laundry with her own, and avoid her parents' questions. On her way home within the runoff, she feeds me crumbs, so I follow her. "Pretty Kolea," she called me one time. "Do you miss your lover? Do you miss your family? Pretty Golden Plover. Soon you will be with them again."

One day at Kahiau's home, I heard her scold her father, "Papa, that's not your T-shirt."

Her father froze, his face stern, "Whose is it?"

Kahiau's mother turned to look from the kitchen where she stirred a pot. Kahiau reddened, but proceeded to tell her father the story of Johnny's dream boat.

"Are you involved with him?" her father asked gruffly when Kahiau finished.

"He doesn't know I exist," Kahiau answered and explained her ritual of taking laundry and returning it. "He pays me for dinners and to do the laundry," Kahiau lied.

Kahiau's father relaxed. "He's leaving on this boat?"

Kahiau nodded. "For the Mainland." She pushed her luck. "He needs fuel to prime the boat motor. I told him we have a spare gas can."

"He's a good customer at the truck. Sell him the one full up for the lawn mower."

Kahiau hugged her father around the neck.

Kahiau's mother relaxed in the kitchen. "How's the boat look?" her mother asked.

"The rudder's secure to the transom. The motor's inboard. He hasn't rigged masts and sails yet. He'll need oars …"

"Those he can find somewhere else." barked Kahiau's father.

Site-Faithful

"Dinner's ready," intercepted Kahiau's mom. "Kahiau, please fill drinks. Papa, call in the children." Kahiau's mother ladled stew into bowls crowded onto a tray with warm rolls covered with a muslin towel. I watched from a perch on the roof next door with sudden longing for my brood.

The next day Kahiau delivered Johnny's laundry and carried the gasoline to the boat. First, palm over palm she stuck closed an open can of paint. Through taped stencils Kahiau deciphered the boat's name— "Dreamcatcher," she whispered. As usual, Johnny lay in a drunken stupor while Kahiau worked to deposit gas into a shiny new motor. If he smelled the gas, the smell didn't revive him. She stole glances at his angular handsome face. As Kahiau's mother described to her father, Kahiau continued to serve as a helpful elf to Johnny's compulsive and drunken shoemaker until an awful day.

One might expect the sky on a day of heart-rending calamity to be storm cloud covered and dark, but the sky on this day was as blue as "a baby boy balloon," as Kahiau described it to her sister that morning. The ruckus began a half mile away from the food wagon and Post Office on the beach. From my perch on the Post Office roof, I could see people standing at the seashore staring in amazement at a beachfront two hundred yards wider as the ocean strangely and suddenly receded leaving some fish flopping on the sand. Some ran toward the ocean, makai, to gather the fish. Some ran toward the mountains, mauka, because they knew that the sea would return in fury, which too soon, happened. I cried out and flew about in frenzy.

Bixby, propped to eat his lunch, was busy tormenting Johnny when a dirty black wave of water knocked Bixby backwards in his chair and dislodged the boat so that Johnny was thrown unconscious on its deck. Bixby couldn't help Johnny because he couldn't help himself, his pale legs flailed as he choked on sandwich and sea water. When the lunch wagon lurched, Kahiau forced open the door and struggled hand over hand along the dislodged wooden fence to reach Johnny. She climbed into the boat. Her weight and the flood water were enough to careen the boat from its base of cinder blocks into the new roiling river that rushed along the storm drain.

When the boat caught the rushing stream in the run-off drain, Johnny sensed the flash forward and started, but was unable to fully rouse himself. Kahiau's soft arm lay against his. "My wife. My wife," Johnny said. Kahiau bent over him, touched his lips with her fingers and whispered, "I'm here. The boat is good. We're good. We're good." Johnny smiled the first smile that I had ever seen on his mouth; then Johnny slept.

I hovered over them and watched helplessly as the boat sprang from side to side of the storm drain scraping against its borders and taking in water. One crash against the wall in a brief tunnel must have broken her finger, but still she remained calm. Kahiau clasped Johnny's head in the strong flesh of her thighs making them one body at the mercy of the crazy see-saw seiche. Forward momentum, after a wild ride, spewed the boat from the storm drain into a cove on an opposing shoreline. She seemed stunned to be free of the raging storm drain current, but after a moment Kahiau started the boat's motor to avoid what was sure to follow—another killing wave. My flock had gathered here to begin our migration to far away Alaska. Kahiau looked up at us and wisely followed toward the safety of deeper water before the boat could spin and collide with rocks on the breakwater. We each escaped in our own fashion. I circled their boat in salute, then joined my kind who fled the chaos on land by commencing our yearly journey north. In my heart I stowed the hope that Kahiau and Johnny, with only wings of wood on water to transport them, could survive.

After a summer of breeding and feeding on the vast rough sponge carpet of the tundra, like all the lucky and the strong, I lived to make another return flight to the island to find that the pangs of death and rebirth had trumped the trivia of scandal. After the tsunami, people on the island recovered, regrouped and even resumed their lives rejuvenated, Kahiau's family among the survivors, Johnny's house and my garden intact.

A new postmaster, Tyrone Goodall, relocated from St. Paul, Minnesota where, he said, "the wind bites." The kiss of trade-winds was a blessing he tasted and marveled at daily. Like Bixby, Tyrone spent his lunch break out of doors with Johnny, but Tyrone helped Johnny weed and harvest fresh vegetables to sell at the food wagon. On this day as Kahiau reached up to hang colorful clothes on the line, her long shiny hair rode the trade winds and shimmered ebony. The warm winds draped her cotton frock against the growing promise of her belly, while Johnny and Tyrone picked the ripest of the tomatoes. "Marry tomato plants with marigolds, Johnny," Tyrone counseled, "and pests'll back off."

I squawked, my pointed wings ruffling, "No worries, sentry Kolea is on surveillance, leave the pests in my emerald garden to me."

Tapping the
Pocket Mirror

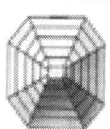

In the interest of healing, Wanda Pickett confided to her Parish priest, Father John Zwirecki that she wanted to learn to play the game that entertained her late husband Andy every Friday night since they'd retired to this island town-- "No Limit Holdem."

For Wanda playing poker was as odd a prospect as being cast at her age as Wonder Woman. How she and Andy laughed about that possibility. He often called Wanda wonder woman for humble homemaking talents, such as crafting soup broth out of "bones and grass," and her miracle way of finding a redeeming grace in "the sourest of curmudgeons." "I'll audition for the remake of Wonder Woman," Wanda teased. "Why not a senior citizen super hero?" Oh, they laughed. "Performing inimitable feats of strength..." Andy said, "while wielding a walker." Since Andy's death Wanda achieved modest feats of strength: getting out of bed each morning, leaving the house, breathing.

She got the idea to play poker while cleaning out Andy's desk. She wasn't cleaning as much as ~~she~~ gleaning pieces of him when she came upon his enveloped stack of eleven $10 bills. He counted his winnings each Friday after the game while she watched from their bed where she lay reading or pretending to be asleep. He'd thumb the bills and mark the current amount on a Post-It.

"If the total goes below $50, I'll skip," Andy said. "If we're flush, I'll play."

Today Wanda pulled $20 from the envelope, smelled the wad of bills as if she might smell Andy on them, kissed them, then folded them back into the envelope and the twenty into her purse to fund her buy-in.

Throwing open her front door and deep breathing

fresh air for ballast, she walked to the driveway, got in and positioned herself on the driver's side of their new Civic hybrid. Friends chauffeured her places since Andy had been rushed by ambulance to the hospital. Today, she'd solo. He was a whole foot taller, so she had to find the controls to draw the seat closer and readjust the mirrors. Doing this simple task initiated a new wave of grief to think that Andy wouldn't be moving the seat back again. Sobbing, she turned on the ignition to listen to the radio, which she quickly changed from country to classical to dodge further associations. She wiped her eyes with copious tissues from a box on the floor and took more deep breaths. She must drive clear-headed. After a calming few minutes, she put the car in reverse, backed out of their gravel driveway and turned onto the road to her new life.

Ever since Andy died, Wanda in her grief had been harvesting static pieces of Andy…memories, scents, mutual appreciations…and stringing them like glass fishing floats onto a mental rope that she trusted to pull her across the ocean of missing him. Poker marked a transition from passive memories to an active one. A memory of Andy that could engage her attention and sail her back into the game of life.

Father Zwirecki, in the role of counselor, approved of the idea of Wanda, Poker Player. "Stop over Friday," Father Zwirecki said. "I'm back playing. I left off a while after my ankle surgery, but I'm playing again Friday." He handed her the address on a torn off scrap of church bulletin. "We're in back of the club. Enter from a side door, Wanda, and you won't have to walk through the bar."

When Wanda opened what she thought must be the correct door, the poker table loomed right inside not fifteen feet away. The players at the table stopped talking when Andy's wife entered the clubroom. Father Zwirecki who'd been anticipating her arrival had his back to her and was at present in a hand. Nobody else at the table acknowledged her presence even though it was her presence that initiated their silence. Andy's sudden death a month ago had penetrated their own cloud of invulnerability whisking them into a face to face showdown with mortality. Andy gone--comrade and fellow poker pirate. A keeper of the camaraderie gone missing.

They all, except maybe Alice, the only female presently at the table, knew who Wanda was from occasional encounters at the grocery store, Movie Theater or Post Office. Wanda knew who Alice was because Andy had described "a red-haired song bird" who sometimes sang Karaoke at the bar with a "real pretty" voice. Andy loved music. Wanda hadn't anticipated that Alice's lovely red hair would be dipped in shocking pink, that her wrists were covered with a collection of gold bracelets, and her arms with Maori tattoos. She was most likely the youngest at the table today. Often, there were young active-duty servicemen, Andy said, but they could be deployed, on duty, or on exercises.

The only two among the poker players who had ever officially met Andy's wife were Hollander and Father Zwirecki. Father knew Andy and Wanda as members of his congregation. Hollander, as Andy's coworker, acted as the trucking company's representative at Andy's funeral. The silence finally compelled Hollander to get up from the table and Father to turn around.

"Mrs. Pickett, Wanda." Father pushed back his chair and leaned on the table to stand. He had to hold onto the chair back because of his recent foot surgery. Wanda saw his crutches stowed against a far wall out of tripping range.

"Father John. Please sit. Don't trouble yourself."

Hollander reached her then. "Wanda. How are you?" he said putting one arm on her shoulder and one at her elbow as if she might fall. Nobody at the table recognized this new soft voice. Hollander seemed to have mutated into a keening undertaker. "Do you remember me?" he crooned, "I worked with Andy. At the funeral I …."

"Sure. I remember."

"What can I do for you, Wanda? Are you meeting friends for lunch? The restaurant is through that sliding divider. Here, I'll open it for you." He started to pressure her ever so gently toward the other room.

Wanda stood her ground. "You're Joe Hollander, right?" Wanda said.

Hollander halted. "I am. I worked in Andy's department."

"Sure. I remember."

"What can I do for you, Wanda," Hollander said at a loss for what to do next.

"I'm here to play, actually."

"Poker? With us?" Hollander morphed back into himself.

"I talked to Father about it. Andy loved this game. I always thought. OK, I'll learn. We'll play together. But I didn't. Ever learn."

"Hey, Wanda. That's OK. It's not important." Truck driver Hollander again turned into Hollander a mollifying Funeral Director.

"Andy played most Fridays," Wanda said.

"That doesn't mean he didn't miss you."

"What? Oh sure. I guess. I just want to see it with his eyes. The game. All of you. It took such a hold of him."

Hollander didn't know what to do or say. It's true they were blinding out a Coastguardsman called back to work. They were playing short tonight. A few players flew to Vegas for a tournament. The active duty guys were absent. "You want to play, Mrs.?" a man she'd heard called Dominico said. He officially ran the game.

"Yes, I do," Wanda said. "Sorry to be late."

"Dutch just got the deal. Sit by him and we'll deal you in on the rest of Craig's chips if that's OK with you.

"I don't know who that is."

In his natural voice, Hollander said, "Dutch's me.

The guys call me Dutch. Come on. Craig's stack is next to mine."

Wanda accepted the Coastguardsman's empty chair and entered the game. She didn't know yet how lucky she was that Andy's game was No Limit Holdem Poker. Her odds of being welcomed into the game were good. Holdem welcomes newbies, as opposed to say Bridge. Poker players, while maintaining a healthy respect for beginner's luck, are glad to have a "fish," an inexperienced player, as another buy-in. Wanda pulled $20.00 from her purse and handed it to Dominico. He tried to refuse it and then to give her change, but Wanda said, "please add it to the pot." Andy often talked about the tournament buy-in price. His policy was not to re-buy even if there was a re-buy option. Dutch clarified the chip values for her— "One hundred, two hundred, five hundred, one thousand."

Any strangeness surrounding Wanda's entering the club and the game was instantly forgotten. Holdem poker flows. Wanda stepped into its current with all the rest. All the players.

"You're lucky, Miss Wanda," Dominico said. "Father's back to keep us on our good behavior."

"I dropped off linens this morning, Father," Wanda said.

"Thank you, Wanda," the priest said. A hospital band encircled Father's wrist. Nurses told him he could cut off the bracelet after his release, but he liked the implication of the words, had referred to them subsequently several times in homilies, and wanted to get full value out of the gentle warning "Fall Risk."

Dutch, aka Hollander, off kilter because of shepherding Wanda, who folded her first hand, made a big move with his own hand and pushed all-in with King Queen suited. Alice on the Big Blind called him with a pair of fours and the fours held up, so Dutch was out.

"Don't I still have a buy in?" Dutch said pushing back his chair.

"No," said Dominico. It's past the first break. You know that."

Dutch pulled his chair in again. "OK. Miss Wanda" Dutch said. "I'm your guru. You know the priority of hands?"

"What?"

"We 'll play together now till you get the hang of it."

Coop, the oldest player at the table with a thick crop of platinum hair, was least rattled by Andy's death. It wasn't that he didn't care for Andy. He missed him a lot. But death seemed to be balanced and held at bay on Coop's shoulders as he walked bent over like a spring wound too tight or a hinge rusted partway open. Coop's blood harbored a slow cancer. "I haven't suffered," he explained to anyone who learned of it. In spite of his ancientness (even these days 89 is old) Coop's mind stayed savvy and sassy.

"Can we have a game tomorrow?" Dutch already pined for another opportunity to play.

"Sorry Bud," Dominico said. "There's a party here tomorrow night. Plus, I got to take my Baby out. Clubbing. Salsa. Gotta keep her happy, you know what I mean? You got Saturday night plans Coop?" Dominico teased the old man.

Coop shot back, "I gotta service two women."

"Ha. There's no excuse for him, Father," Dominico said.

"That's OK," said Father John, then he broke the ensuing awkward silence with a story. "The other day a group of maybe three, four Coeds stopped by the rectory and asked the housekeeper to see me. I went to greet them by the Parish entryway. I said, 'Hello Ladies. May I help you?' Very polite, the lead girl says, 'Father, we're on a scavenger hunt.'

"'Fun, what are you looking for?'" I said.

The first girl hesitated. Another girl stepped forward. 'Father,' this girl said, 'we need to take a selfie of all of us with a six-foot male virgin.'

"Oh my God. Oops. I mean what did you tell them, Father?" Alice asked him.

"I told them I couldn't help them."

The table was silent.

"I'm only five ten," Father said.

"Hah." Coop said. The other men laughed as did Alice and Wanda. Wanda felt she hadn't laughed in a very long while.

"Father John, you're a hoot," Alice said. "I might have to come back to church."

"Door's literally always open," Father said. "I raise," he said and bet twice the blind.

Coop folded.

"Call," Dutch instructed Wanda, so she did.

Dominico called, too. So did Alice. "What's happening here?" Alice said.

On the board the flop came down ten of spades, ten of hearts and Queen of hearts. Wanda was playing King of hearts and Jack of hearts.

"Do you know what you have?" Dutch asked her.

"Not much yet," Wanda said. She looked at her hand.

"Sh-h-h. Bet," Dutch said. He found playing another's chips exhilarating.

Wanda bet twice the blind. Then she started when Alice called her. Alice with Ace of spades, ten of clubs.

Father called the raise with Ace of hearts, Queen of spades.

"What do you people have?" Dominico folded bitterly.

The turn card was the nine of hearts giving Wanda the straight flush Dutch deemed worth chasing with Wanda's chips.

"Oh," Wanda said too quickly then followed Dutch's suggestion that she check.

Alice noticed Wanda's tell and checked. Father checked.

The river card was the queen of clubs.

Wanda knew to check this time.

Alice went all-in.

"Like Thomas, I've got to see it," Father went all-in thinking he had them.

Wanda, of course, called the all-in thinking Andy must be helping her.

"I've got a boat," Alice said. Tens full of queens."

"I've got a higher boat," said Father showing his Queens full of tens.

"Wanda's got a straight flush, Ladies and Gentlemen," Dutch said, and Wanda showed the King and Jack of Hearts.

"Talk about your beginner's luck." Dominico said, "Time for a break."

"Take a picture before you muck," Alice yelled and grabbed what she thought was a smartphone camera from the front pouch of Wanda's purse.

"Oh, that's a pocket mirror," Wanda told Alice. I know it looks like a phone. My grandbaby taps at it thinking it's a touchscreen."

"Ha. Tapping the pocket mirror. That's ambitious. There's an idea in there for Apple. A secret mirror/camera phone. Here," Alice said, "fan the cards." and she snapped a photo from her own phone. "This'll be your Christmas card. I'll text it to you."

"Twenty minutes' break," Dominico said. "I'm hungry."

"Where's the ladies' room?" Wanda said.

"Here I'll show you and finish texting the photo. You have a smartphone?"

Wanda nodded. They had to leave the building and reenter another door. A lot of the smokers walked outside, too. Father John headed to the bar with Coop who had fetched Father's crutches.

"Alice, eh? Alice in Wonderland," Wanda said, "was my nickname in high school."

"Mine, too," Alice said.

"I was shy," Wanda said.

"I was Alice." Alice still held Wanda's mirror. "Actually, my mom named me 'Singer.' I use my middle name Alice. My last name is 'Young,' and my mom wanted my name whenever attendance was called to be 'Young, Singer.' I got embarrassed so I used Alice. Can I borrow your pocket mirror a minute?"

"Sure, keep it. I hardly have a use for it anymore. There's a strange little old lady in it these days."

Alice held the mirror up, smiled, then handed it back to Wanda. "All clear. How come we've never met you before? I didn't even know Andy had a wife."

Wanda started.

"I mean he never mentioned you."

Wanda didn't say anything.

"I mean I only knew him from poker."

Wanda laughed. "I'm not jealous. Are you married, Alice?"

"My husband's on a submarine."

"That must get lonely."

"Sometimes. Like everybody. Sometimes I'm lonely. I got married late. I knew what I was in for. The military, I mean. Some ladies can't hack it. A lot of moving, a lot of goodbyes and needing to make new friends. Finding jobs."

"I'm sure that's true," Wanda said. "Does your husband play poker? When he's in port?"

Alice grunted. "No. He hates Poker. Says it's the nastiest dirtiest meanest card game there is. I disagree with him. There's a kind of sweet etiquette to it. Like sea lore."

"Sea lore?"

"Well, I mean, when you're on a boat there's an etiquette. Special words to say like 'Ahoy' and 'anchors aweigh.' In poker, if you lose a hand. It's polite to say 'good hand.' If you go out it's polite to shake hands with the winner. Good hand, by the way." Alice reached out to shake Wanda's hand. "When people don't take losing personally, there's an honor to being at a table with lots of action. I think the guys respect me as a player. I like that. Being a player. To me that's more important than winning. Why are you here?"

"What? Oh, I wanted to learn the game Andy enjoyed so much. I asked him to teach me, but he said I was too soft. I guess he meant that as a compliment. Some Wonder Woman. He called me that, too."

"I like that in a husband that he called you Wonder Woman. You did great so far."

"Thanks. With Dutch's help. Maybe with Andy's help."

"You don't need anybody's help. Come back. It would be good to have more women at the table."

"I won't make them sad missing Andy?"

"You'll make yourself happy."

"Yeah. I guess. I'll be happy. Again."

"You will."

A wild sob escaped the chains of inhibition Wanda thought she'd locked shut. "It's a double whammy getting old and losing someone you love so much."

Alice with her red and shocking pink hair, said very softly for her, "You don't have to be old to lose someone, Wanda."

"You?"

Alice nodded.

"Your parents, a sibling?"

Alice shook her head. "I'm an only child."

"Oh. A child."

"Bingo."

"A baby."

"Yes, Ma'am."

"Miscarriage?"

"Yes, Ma'am. A loss that nobody sees, but me."

"Your husband…"

"He missed it. Was deployed. Which is a blessing in a way."

"How long ago?"

"One year. I still count missed milestones."

"I'm sorry, Alice."

"Thank you, Wanda. See we have a lot in common. More than these Guys need to know."

Alice handed the pocket mirror back to Wanda. "You should keep it. Pocket mirrors are important. Like in the TV shows, the girl takes out her pocket mirror, bends it in the sunlight… Flash! The passing pilot gets a signal from the wilderness. Lost person saved."

One of the guy's voices called from outside. "Break's over."

Alice said. "Go on back and take more chips."

"You're not coming back?"

"You took me out, Wanda. Wonder Woman and her straight flush."

"I'm sorry."

"Don't be sorry. Father would have beat me anyhow."

"Are you sure you wouldn't like to keep the pocket mirror, Alice?" She held it out to the younger woman. "I don't much like to look at the old lady in there."

Alice took hold of the mirror and studied it. "I don't see any little old lady."

"Of course you don't."

"No. I mean it. Here look again. Look." Alice held up the mirror.

Wanda shook her head and turned away.

"Wanda look. The mirror bluffs. You have to call the mirror's bluff. Here." Alice held the mirror up to Wanda's face. "Look. Look at her. I see Wonder Woman Wanda, poker player."

Wanda looked and smiled.

"See. She's pleased with herself. Giant killer Wanda. She wants to play some more, doesn't she?"

"Yes, she does."

"Good …," Alice said. And she tucked and patted the pocket mirror back into Wanda's purse. "…cause you're still in and you have a MOUNTAIN of chips to protect."

The Green Umbrella

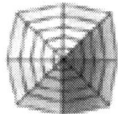

When Lil's soft hand gripped Joe's on the steering wheel at the stop sign, Joe caught the lingering scent of the maile lei she had draped over Andrew's framed photograph. "Wait," Lil said, "for the cute lady."

Joe waited and they watched an old woman step into the street. The woman's face, her mouth weighed down by a survived stroke, betrayed any possible intended show of gratitude or social pleasantry. Only heavy-lidded almond eyes fluttered with recognition of a path secured for her to venture into the street.

The Green Umbrella

"Your cute lady's giving me a dirty look," Joe said.

"I don't think it's for you," Lil said. "I think she has a hard time."

Slowly and with difficulty the tiny old woman, her body twisted and retracted with age, crossed in front of them. Her gait was surer on the left side than the right because she leaned on the polished wooden handle of a handsome green silk umbrella. She tossed her parted cropped white hair and bent body forward taking tiny shuffle steps with disproportionately large trawler shoes to catch up to the planted umbrella support. It took her some time to cross.

"Hawaii has the tiniest people in the world and the hugest," Lil said. "Sparrows and Amazons."

"I'll give you that Samoans are big people," Joe said, "...and some Filipinos are slight. She looks Japanese."

"Yup. We're all from far away. Even Hawaiians."

"'Amazons and Sparrows.' You think of the damnedest things." The old lady hefted one sturdy shoe up onto the curb. Joe hesitated, then turned the corner, and glanced at Lil through a veil of sunshine. "By the way, what did you say to Andrew's mother at the memorial service? I was standing with Master Chief and the Commander and I looked over. She hugged you so fast I thought you'd both fall down."

Lil looked away out the window on her side. "I said… my brother John died in that way, too, and that you said it was like a hydrogen bomb going off in the family." Her eyes teared up.

"Oh."

They drove on around the block. When they reached an open parking space near the end of the street in their neighborhood, which was an overcrowded mass of sterile cube-shaped apartment buildings, small sugar cane cottages and an eclectic mix of modern single and multi-family dwellings, the old lady had just reached a crosswalk in front of them. Again she placed a heavy shoe into the street and, leaning on the umbrella, hobbled across step by vigilant step. She reminded Lil of the ubiquitous cattle egrets when they walk, how they thrust out their snowy heads and plod forward lifting and planting wide feet. When they fly, they're fleeting white star arrows, pointed wings flapping, white breasts pushing at the sky to make it notice their freedom. Lil imagined that it would be easier and more graceful for the old lady, too, if she could fly, but she can't. People can't. At the most, they can see, hear, smell, feel. "I thought she'd stop at the bus stop," Lil said. "At least to rest."

"Tenacious," Joe said. "And grumpy. But hey if I were that old, I'd be grumpy, too."

"Sometimes you're grumpy anyway."

"Never." Joe backed into the space.

"Grumpy's better than sad," Lil said.

"Are you sad my love?" asked Joe. He pulled out the keys and turned to give her words, which he understood to be laden with grief, his full attention.

"Oh, I'm thinking of Andrew. And my brother, John. Both of them young, movie star good looking. John could have gotten paid for being as funny as he was. Andrew at the clinic, well they both, cared so much." She ventured a glance at Joe. "I was away at school one time and needed money. John, he was just a little boy, sent me $5 and eleven cents taped to a piece of Good & Plenty box." Lil smiled. "It was all the money he had. I don't know. And Andrew was never too busy to escort patients through the maze of offices and waiting rooms. Both of them the last people you'd…"

Joe knew she'd cry if they kept talking, he'd been worried about her getting through today, so he got out and walked around to take her arm as they climbed the few stone steps to their first-floor apartment in silence. Sudden raindrops plashed from out of the still sunny sky onto their skin and clothes.

They took their shoes off inside the door. Joe held his in one hand. He leaned in toward Lil and kissed her cheek catching the scent of the lei again. "I'm changing out of this uniform pronto," he said and headed to the bedroom.

"I'll brew some of the good green tea," Lil said. She walked into the kitchen, lifted the kettle from the stove and went to turn on the tap to fill it. From the sliding window over their sink she had a clear view of a lime green patch of Liliuokalani Botanical Garden and beyond that to the next street over and beyond that to a grayed-out fringe of mountains where soon the glow of a rainbow would appear like a spritely film projection.

Lil saw that the rain blew in sheets now pulsing across unkempt grass and roiling fuchsia bougainvillea blossoms. Wind and rain washed high over two royal palms in the park whose frond heads swayed and twirled with the solemn dignity of the ages. Rain began to spray into the kitchen through the window they had left open this morning. Lil reached with her free hand and slid it shut. At the same time she noticed and recognized entering the framed landscape in the lower right-hand corner a familiar uneven gait topped by a large circle of green proceeding slowly but steadily along the far sidewalk against the downfall.

Lil let the kettle clunk down into the sink unfilled and took hold of the porcelain edge with both hands to steady herself. She groaned.

Hearing the wrong clang of the kettle falling, Joe hurried in. "Are you OK?" He turned her to him and she let his t-shirted shoulder be the breaker for a tsunami of tears.

When she could breathe and speak, she said, "I wish they had some kind of help like that and they didn't have any. I wish they could see it now and they can't see it. They can't anymore."

"What baby," Joe said. "See what?"

She looked toward and through their window's

percussion of tears. "I just wish that John and Andrew could see her green umbrella open in the rain."

MILITARY

SANKSHUERY

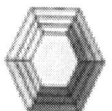

Will Pollack's "wandering foot," along with encouragement from his father, "that's bankable experience," led Will to join the Army. While on active duty, Will traveled from Jersey to Georgia to the Middle East and back nine times. Honorably discharged from Army Infantry after his final deployment, Will needed to draw on this experience to rejoin nonmilitary life. He sat filling out applications at a cramped NJ State Employment Office.

Across the crowded table, a huge, dark-haired guy wearing a plaid shirt unbuttoned over a T-shirt that read

Sankshuery

"S-a-n-k-s-h-u-e-r-y" across his chest bolted up from between two average-sized people, shuffled papers together, and left. Will watched him dodge traffic like a tight end running the ball and walk into a fast food restaurant. Good idea, Will thought, that place has wireless, too. He closed his laptop, selected several job applications, and followed, but Will crossed with the walk signal because his left leg, having been crushed by an IED, dragged.

He entered the restaurant. "One large coffee, please." He spotted the big guy pen-in-hand at an empty table. "Make that two." They won't throw out customers.

Will balanced a tray on his laptop, raked onto it sugar and cream packets, yanked out dispensered napkins, and walked over.

"This seat open?" Will set the tray down and offered a coffee. "On me, Bro. All I want is wireless and table space. It appears we're in the same boat."

The sad, keen eyes of the giant who fled the Employment Office assessed Will's laptop and blank applications. "I guess. Thanks."

They resumed filling out forms until behind Will's back a server cracked the ratchet hook of a window and swished it open. Will, knocking over his chair with a crash, pushed away from the bolted table jolting the coffees, wheeled about and settled on one knee in combat stance positioning a phantom weapon.

The man he'd followed stared down at him as did the few inside customers, the servers, and the manager—everyone in stop motion.

"Been deployed?" the big guy blotted spilled coffee with napkins.

"Yup," said Will. He stood, rearranged the chair, reached for the soiled napkins, and trashed them, along with a ruined application.

Up front, owl eyes glued on them, the manager waved an all-clear, and servers resumed working.

The big guy repositioned Will's laptop, hovering at the table's edge, and retrieved Will's pen from a chair seat. "'A' or 'I'?" he said.

"Yeah, both."

The dark-haired man extended his huge hand. "Thank you for your service. I'm Charlie. Charlie Castor."

"Will Pollack." Will felt the guy trembling. "Jesus, you OK? Sorry to startle you, man."

Charlie Castor steadied his hands on the table. "No, I'm not—OK, but not because of you."

Will sat down. "What's wrong?"

Charlie's face twisted, his voice rasped, "Aw, I'm filling out these damn applications for jack shit."

"There's gotta be jobs, man. It'd be illegal or something."

Charlie curled his hands into fists. "No jobs for me just out of the tank—prison." He nodded toward the employment office. "Any of them'll be hired first."

Will couldn't bring himself to toss Charlie a niggling platitude —You'll find something—There's a job with your name on it—something'll turn up.

Charlie snorted a laugh. "Without my full meds…" He lifted taser hands.

"Meds?"

"Inside I got diagnosed bi-polar and treated," he said, "I could function. Now, no job, no insurance, no meds."

"There's community clinics, online insurance, Social Security," Will said, feeling as if he dangled Band-Aids at a man bleeding to death.

Charlie Castor sat elbows bent, fists curled, eyes partly closed, like a blind lion statue. "Friggin paperwork."

Will persisted, "OK then, you work in prison, Charlie?"

"Road crew, silkscreen… sometimes loading detail."

"That's all bankable experience," Will said. "How'd you wind up inside anyhow?"

"I set fire to my professor's house when he recommended kicking me out of school. One week to a degree. Caught in the act, thank God."

"Jesus." Will glanced outside at a girl struggling briefly to right a rolling suitcase that flipped over when she left the curb. He looked back at Charlie. "Degree in what?"

"Counseling."

Both men laughed.

"I can't spell," Charlie said, "so--- I failed his final. And I'm sick, crazy. He knew. I didn't."

"It's not your fault if you're sick."

"Like whose fault it is matters. It's not your fault you freaked a while ago."

Will Pollack remembered the freewheeling wanderlustful boy who enlisted in the Army. Now he was a man with a gimp leg and a troubled mind, but one who bonded with strangers fighting similar battles. He'd had this bankable experience embossed on him under searing pressure as on a coin. Even the ugly face of war could have a flip side.

Suddenly, the restaurant jingle blurted out from a background speaker, "BA-DA-BA-BA-BA."

As if it signaled reveille, Will took charge. To Will, he and Charlie comprised a unit with a mission. "OK. We're doing this. Here. Every Day. Until we get something," Will said.

Charlie stared at Will already writing, shook his head, steadied trembling hands, and started on another application, occasionally asking Will to spell a word.

Runaway Train

I'm Toby's younger sister by a year and a half. We both still live at home because of this economy, which sucks. The economy, I mean. Living at home's not so bad. We talk. Toby tells me stuff, the important stuff. It's not like he doesn't have friends. He does, but he's hot-headed and not easy to get along with since finishing up his last deployment in Afghanistan. Mom says he's forgotten how to talk day to day nice to people. He's like revved up so she's asked me to kind of look after him. To keep him out of trouble and calm him down. Sometimes that's like trying to stop a runaway train.

Don't get me wrong. He's got a heart of gold. He'd walk hot coals for friends and family. Especially for an Army buddy. In this case, the soldier of which I'm speaking was already dead.

Saturdays, Toby and I go to breakfast because mom works weekends, and our dad sleeps in that one day. This Saturday, I was looking to go, I'd already decided to have whip cream on IHOP Blueberry waffles, but I find Toby by the bathroom mirror dressed in his uniform and shaving. In uniform. Uh-oh. I sit down on the tub. "What's up?"

"I gotta do something," Toby says. "I gotta go to a wedding." He taps his razor on the sink and the lather slithers off like hairy whip cream. Toby rinses it down the drain– the only whip cream I'm seeing today I figure. "You can come if you want. It's in Wilkes Barre."

"Who do we know in Wilkes Barre?"

"Oh—it's about a guy from my unit."

"It's about?"

"Look, if you're coming, get dressed. I'll tell you the whole story in the car."

I've been itching to wear the plum colored tea-length formal I got 75% off. "Ok, 20 minutes."

In the car Toby tells me the whole story, and I start to sweat.

He says, "All I'm gonna do is at the part where they ask does anyone know any reason why this couple shouldn't get married, I'm gonna say they shouldn't because the bride loves Fulton, my friend."

"Isn't Fulton the guy who got killed? The IED? You missed his funeral by a month you told me?"

"He died ten weeks ago. Her getting married right now is an insult. Look, Fulton loved this girl more than his own life." He bangs his hands on the steering wheel a couple times. "This is just not right."

I'm wishing I'm driving instead of Toby. He's out of practice. I can't watch him brake so late, so I look out the window and start thinking about this wedding, about the girl. She's on the rebound maybe. Maybe she knew all along Fulton wasn't the one, but I don't say that out loud cause I don't want to make Toby more mad. Anyhow, this is her wedding day. I'm thinking about her parents, all the arrangements—the flowers, the relatives. What will they think if Toby stands up in uniform and says something crazy? I look over at him. "This is crazy. Toby, you don't know her."

Jesus. He's looking like he's going to cry. Only time I saw him cry was at Little League ten years ago when his little finger jutted out at an odd angle. I'm feeling sorry I said anything. Finally—he like gulps and whispers, "I'm doing it for Fulton." I shut up.

We get to the church. Turns out Toby knows the Best Man, another guy from their unit. Toby introduces me and they talk a little. Toby doesn't mention what he's going to do.

We're ushered to our seats on the bride's side. Toby's decision. He doesn't want anything to do with the groom.

I say I have to go to the bathroom. I find the Best Man, tell him what Toby's plan is and sit back down.

Next thing I know a guy comes and whispers to Toby that the Best Man wants to see him outside. Oh God. I follow them out.

The Best Man says to Toby. "I can't let you do this, man. You don't know the whole story."

Toby gives me stink eyes and says to the Best Man, "I'm doing it for Fulton.

"What all can you do for Fulton now, huh?" The Best Man takes a hold of Toby's shoulders—a little too hard. "Fulton's dead."

Toby yells back at him, "Fulton loved her, man."

"She loved him."

Toby shakes free. "So how can she marry this guy so soon?" Toby's red-faced now and to hush him up cause all these dressed-up guests are pouring past us into the church, the Best Man muscles him over and out of the way beside the church garage. Oh shit.

"Listen to me," the Best Man is saying. "Listen to me." He's pushing Toby at the chest. Toby's so mad at me; I'm thinking how'll I find another way home.

"Just listen to me," the Best Man hollers. He leans over and whispers by Toby's ear. "She's pregnant. With Fulton's kid."

Toby backs into a wall and sits. The wind gone out of him. "So, who's the guy she's marrying?"

The Best Man sits alongside him. "A friend from the neighborhood." He blinks. "He's cool with it, man." I can tell Toby's thinking about that. The Best Man says, "This is for Fulton's baby, man. You gotta let this happen. Don't raise the dead here. Not at a wedding." He puts his hand on Toby's shoulder and rocks him. "What can you do for Fulton now? What can anybody do for Fulton now, man. Fulton's out of the picture."

Toby shakes him off then, jumps up and flicks the whole wedding idea away with the back of his hand. "I don't have to watch," he says.

"Right. It's best you leave." The Best Man stands and holds his arm out towards the parking lot like he's a traffic cop.

Toby goes off in a huff. At least he's not bleeding. I watch. He's not looking back for me. I have no ride. No money. Right now, Toby hates me. My plum dress is perfect, though—for a wedding.

So, I go to the wedding, but I sit on the groom's side out of sympathy for what he's doing, whether he really knows about the entire situation or he's in the dark.

Toby isn't there at that question raising part, so the bride marries the friend from the neighborhood.

Afterwards, the Best Man invites me to the reception and promises he'll see I get there and home OK. What the heck. I can't go home yet. Toby'll kill me. I ride over with Mr. and Mrs. Swenski, the Best Man's aunt and uncle. Mr. Swenski says, "Where's your friend? I saw you with a young fellow in uniform."

"Toby's my brother," I say, and I explain that Toby's friend died in the war and tell the Swenski's why he's especially upset today. That might have been another mistake. I won't get any prizes for keeping my mouth shut today. Mr. Swenski goes all quiet. "Mr. Swenski's a veteran, too," Mrs. Swenski says turning to look at me, "Viet Nam."

The hotel ballroom looks beautiful. There's about ten big round tables covered in white with about ten chairs at each table. Each chair's covered in white with a live calla lily and white satin bow attached to the back of it. I'm wishing I had my phone to show Mom.

I sit with the Swenski's. I'm glad I stayed, so far.

After all the bouquet throwing and garter and everything when people are pretty much just dancing, who shows up, but my brother—shit-faced. Toby staggers over, looks me and my dancing partner, the Best Man, in the eye, hands me his uniform hat, then lays down smack in the middle of the dance floor.

"What're you doing, man?"

Runaway Train

Toby raises his fist. He's crying dammit.

Mr. Swenski sees him and stops dancing, too. Mrs. Swenski pulls her husband at the arm, but Mr. Swenski goes over by Toby. He's gets down on his hands and knees and he says kind of loud to Toby, "I'm a vet, too, son." Next thing they're both laying there side by side on the floor like stripes. I sit down again at our table.

Mrs. Swenski ~~kind of~~ wrings her hands, shrugs, ~~and~~ waddles back and sits down again at the table with me. The Best Man and his buddies drag some calla lily chairs around Toby and Mr. Swenski and let them stay there. Yeah, I dance. A lot. I'm lovin' life. dance after dance like some kind of crazy monument. Mrs. Swenski comes over to hand me Toby's hat and to get her husband when the band cuts out and the music is ended for the night. Mr. Swenski gets up, but Toby's too shit-faced. Mrs. Swenski and I follow along to the parking lot as Mr. Swenski and the Best Man brace Toby on their shoulders to get him into the back seat of our car. They strap him in. The Best Man takes Toby's hat out of my hands, puts it on my head, and kisses my cheek. I drive home.

Plummet and Shine

Bypassing the rest stop on Interstate 40, Cole sought out a coffee shop on the old Route 66. He wanted to step back in time, to taste oven-warm pie baked by the person who serves it, to get a buzz from unchained coffee, and to trace for a few miles the "Mother Road." When he left home he had four days of Emergency Leave remaining. He had set out on an illogical odyssey to find the site where fifteen years ago his mother told him a story.

On that day fifteen years ago he was a sweating cranky ten-year-old forced to leave yet another posse of

Plummet and Shine

friends. He sat seat-belted into the rear of the jammed full family van feeling like uninventoried household goods. Along the seemingly endless road to his dad's next duty station at Twenty-Nine Palms, he remembered coming upon a graphic billboard cartoon of a massive meteor plummeting toward the blue marble of planet Earth. "AWESOME!" He'd struggled to turn around in his seat-belt prison to read about it.

His mother, thrilled that he'd stopped pouting, told him that about fifty thousand years ago, a crashing meteor punched a one-mile-wide hole in the earth near Canyon Diablo, Arizona. "No human would have witnessed the event," she said. "But when humans did come along, it astounded them," she continued. "And more than a hundred years ago, a Nobel prize-winning French chemist, Ferdinand Henri Moissan scraped and examined the crater's guts and discovered mineral fragments of Stardust," her eyes twinkling when she turned to pin into his brain and heart the magic of the word "stardust." Since Cole's family didn't pause to visit the landmark that day, today Cole decided on a plan to find the place and throw his mother's ring into the crater. His plan had a logic imposed by grief and frustration.

The Hashknife Diner and Souvenir Shop smelled sweetly of cherries, more than likely some form of the tax-free tobacco offerings Cole reasoned. Cole sat on a round counter swivel stool and ordered a slice of home-made Sweet Potato pie and a cup of coffee. After a few minutes, a man disguised as a Joe Tourist, wearing a "Good Fellas Bail Bonds, Las Vegas, Nevada" hoodie pulled up over a ball cap, mirrored sunglasses and holding a map, sauntered over, "Say Bud, how do I get to Joseph City?"

"Sorry, Sir, I'm not from around here."

The man grunted and dropped the map in front of Cole's stool. When Cole bent over to help retrieve it, he felt the man's hand bump his back pocket. Cole spun around on the counter seat, grabbed the would-be pickpocket by the wrist and employed a Tai Chi strike technique he'd learned in the service. Cole whispered into the jerk's ear, "Hit the road. NOW—or your next rest stop will be the ER." As the imposter backed away brushing off his arm to make as if Cole had assaulted him, Cole noted the man wore expensive black and red Nike running shoes. Cole had little time to reach the crater and didn't make the effort to report the incident. Mistake.

Almost as soon as Cole left the diner, he came upon a billboard like the one he remembered seeing as a boy and shortly afterwards he finally reached the roadside attraction and educational research center named Meteor Crater off of Interstate 40.

A few moments later, while standing at the massive crater's rim, Cole debunked a plan to fling his ill-fated engagement ring, his mother's wedding ring, into the crater—dust to dust. Standing poised to throw the ring away, he looked around him and begrudged the parking lot, the steep admission charge, a gift shop, a nearby RV trailer park—all-in-all the micro-management of a natural wonder. If Cole did pitch the ring into the crater, he imagined a hiking Joe Tourist, or maybe the punk who tried to rob him, picking up the ring, wiping it off and examining it, and boasting that its sale might just cover the cost of road trip gas or a Vegas gambling spree. No. The crater didn't offer a fit enough ending for Cole's engagement story; no matter how fit a metaphor for the gaping hole in his heart. He whispered into the wind, "I finally got to see it, Mom. Your diamond place."

Needing a new plan, Cole recalled seeing among the gaudy signs along the old and legendary Route 66 advertising Trading Posts, Wigwams, lucky Jackalope antlers, petrified wood, and authentic Navajo rugs, an odd sign which reminded him of the kind of ads you'd see for fortune tellers: "**Transform Your Heartache 10 miles—Miss Ruth De Leonne**." Was someone reading his mind? He yearned to transform this searing lava flow of misery into something bearable.

Cole calculated 5 miles to go to reach the "transforming" service advertised like a muffler repair shop. Soon he spotted another sign with the same font and design: "**Transform Your Heartache 2 ½ miles—Miss Ruth De Leonne**." True or bogus an actual place and person advertised relief. God bless America and Route 66!

Just two miles past the town of Two Guns he entered a near ghost town of shops with boarded windows. Rerouting the highway to the interstate had taken a toll. Within the town's 25 MPH zone another sign in the same style read "**You've Gone Too Far—Miss Ruth De Leonne**." Cole turned his bike around. In the window of an open barber shop hung a similar sign that he'd missed

before because of an 18-wheeler parked on the street—
"**Look Higher**." He looked above the shop and there in one window— "**Transform Your Heartache Here—Miss Ruth De Leonne**."

Cole parked and entered the barber shop on the front of which swirled an old-fashioned barber pole. A wiry-haired barber stood with comb and scissors in hand trimming the crown of a be-caped truck driver type, maybe the driver of the 18-wheeler parked in front. Two other men and a mom with a mop-headed little boy waited on worn red leather seats.

"Excuse me," Cole said.

"Up there." The barber pointed with his scissors. "Easy as white rice. Push the buzzer on the side door. Open and call up. Loud and lucid y'hear. She's elderly."

"How did you know why I'm here?"

"Salmon come to Capistrano, right? I heard your cycle pass and sally back. And… Do…You… Need a Haircut? No." He resumed snipping, "…if you wanted a haircut, you've stopped at the first pass, and when you came in you'd sit…" he nodded at an empty seat… "and eyeball how many folks are waiting." He snapped his scissors. "I know folks. I know what makes 'em tick. You, my high and tighty friend, are here to see Miss Ruth."

Cole didn't like being "known" by any wily barber. He did look at the folks waiting then, and he thought when the barber announced that Cole was here to see Miss Ruth they eyed him back sizing him up. Small town thing, Cole decided.

"Thanks." Cole turned to leave.

"You're more than welcome, but less than delighted," the barber chuckled.

With half a mind to jump on his bike and split, Cole sauntered back outside, identified the side entrance and stared at it bothered by misgiving, but motivated by despair. Finally, he walked over and thumbed the buzzer. He tried the door—unlocked. He peered up at another door at the top of the stairs which was ajar and yelled, "Hell OH." He started when an old woman's voice crooned through an intercom at his ear like one of those animated shoulder perched angels in cartoons. She said, "Come up, son. You're welcome here." He decided to ignore the devil on his other shoulder that looked and sounded a lot like the scissors wielding barber.

Cole climbed the creaky stairs and pulled aside a lace curtain to enter a tidy living room. A silver-haired African American woman sat in a cushioned armless rocker with a red white and blue wedding ring quilt spread over her lap. On a small table sat a large mouthed jar labeled "$10.00 fee/donation" in between Cole and a ladder-back chair next to the old woman's. She could be a hundred years old, Cole thought. He reached for his wallet, extracted a $10 bill and pushed it into the jar.

"Thank you, son." Miss Ruth closed a worn leather Bible.

Cole entered the room, his sun-shocked eyes led by the dim flame of an antique train lantern, which smelled faintly of kerosene. More lace panels twirled like background dancers over the artificial breeze of a window air conditioner.

"Rest, Son. Let go the road." She indicated the empty chair "Tea or coffee?"

Cole sat down placing his helmet on the floor. "Coffee, I guess. Please, Ma'am."

"Coffee, Clement. Two please. Have Carol bring them," she spoke quietly into a variable intercom speaker postured near her bony fingertips.

The barber's voice fuzzed, "On it, Miss Ruth. Quick as Mickey Dee's."

"What brings you, son?" She patted the Bible, its wrinkled black skin as amiably worn as her own.

"I want to feel better, Ma'am."

"Soldier, am I correct?"

"How'd you tell, Ma'am?"

"Short hair in a long hair town. Too many soldiers these days, too many wars, goin on too long. Anyhow, son, what's your story?"

"For one thing, I brought a ring to throw into the canyon."

"The canyon? Hah. Mostly fellows or girls throw away rings into the Little Colorado River by Winslow."

"So many throw away rings?"

"Enough and too many. What's your story, son?"

"Well, Ma'am. I feel I need to talk to somebody."

The old woman's warm fingertips touched the top of Cole's hand, "Please. Call me Miss Ruth."

"Miss Ruth—my father was military, too, like me— We'd be ALWAYS on the road. We passed by this same canyon when I was young on our way to Twenty-Nine Palms…" Miss Ruth nodded.

A soft "Hey folks." at the door interrupted them.

"Coffee first. Come in, Carol. Thanks."

The mother of the mop-headed boy seated downstairs pushed aside the curtain with a tray holding a Mr. Coffee pot, mugs, spoons, sugar cubes piled in a topless Blue Willow sugar bowl, and a creamer sweating from cold.

A pleasant lemony perfume entered with the girl. Her jeans were worn pale and the white cotton shirt she had on was too big for her so she'd rolled the sleeves up at the cuff exposing long unadorned wrists and clean graceful hands with no nail polish. Cole sighed to see a thin gold band on the third finger of her left hand. She set down the tray and pushed back long bronze hair. "May I stay up here for a few, Miss Ruth? Drew's getting a haircut."

Miss Ruth looked to Cole. "I don't mind. Sure," he said. He wanted to wade in the young woman's perfume and feathery voice.

"Carol this is Cole Baker."

"How'd you like your coffee, Cole?"

To his specifications, Carol plopped in sugar, stirred in cream, and handed mugs around, carefully settling Miss Ruth's on the side table clear of the Bible.

Cole stood and offered her his seat, but Carol waved him off and sat on her hands on the edge of Miss Ruth's bed. Clearing his throat, Cole continued after Miss Ruth nodded. "… long ago my mom told me a story about here."

"Here?" Carol said.

Cole nodded. "My mom, she and dad recently—twelve days ago—passed away—accident." Cole swallowed "Car accident..."

Carol brought her hand to her mouth. "Oh God, I'm so sorry." Miss Ruth shook her head. Cole took a deep breath. "Yeah, funny, they worried over me—at war, and I was the one who got the bad news." Miss Ruth shook her head once again. Cole gripped the seat of his chair. "Anyhow, my mom loved---science. She told me that natural moissanite, which is what this ring is made of..." Cole pulled the ring from his wallet and passed it to Miss Ruth who passed it to Carol who passed it back… "was discovered in this canyon by here."

Cole held the ring up to show off the gemstone. "The story as my mom actually told me was that a smart man, a genius, a scientist—in France, invented a new kind of furnace. He dreamed of making diamonds. More than a hundred years ago he traveled to America to examine the site of a gigantic crater formed in ancient times by a meteor crashing into the earth…"

"Meteor Crater," Carol said.

"Yes…He had a hunch that the disaster of terrific heat and pressure concentrated in one spot must have produced something extraordinary." Cole flushed.

Miss Ruth pointed over her head and Carol stood up and pulled the dangling silk-tasseled cord of a ceiling fan birthing a whir and breeze that inspired new dips and turns in the dancing lace curtains.

Miss Ruth rocked back and forth a little and adjusted the quilt high up to her shoulders underlining the palpable compassion conveyed by brown velvet eyes. "He found diamonds?"

"Not quite," Cole cleared his throat, which had tightened more than he anticipated. "Near and about the crater he discovered a new mineral. Like nothing found naturally to that point on earth. He reasoned the mineral was the result of the exploded star that plummeted to earth."

"My son Drew'd like this story," Carol said.

"Hah. You mean a star's the meteor? I disremember science class."

"Yes Ma'am. Anyway my mom called it a star."

"How did you get a ring made of this stuff?" Carol asked.

"After she told the story, my mom showed me her engagement ring. It took a long while, my mother said, but finally, scientists, right here in America, synthetically produced gems of this mineral that rival natural diamonds. Now the stone is called Moissanite in honor of Henri Moissan, the scientist who lifted the natural mineral from the crater."

Miss Ruth touched Cole's arm. "In all my years I have never heard that story. Thank you, son."

"It's a great story," Carol said.

"My mom's story about the man who discovered jewels in stardust stuck with me." Cole shifted in his chair. "Just about five months before I lost my parents—" He looked at Carol. "… I got engaged. Short story short, she accepted the ring. I deployed. I've deployed four times. She met a local guy, a pharmacist, and sent me back the ring in a Thank You card. Well, a No Thank You card."

"The ring is still special to you," Carol said. Miss Ruth sipped her coffee.

"Sure. Well, sure. It was my mom's. From my dad. And I figure moissanite is as close to an American diamond there could be. I like that idea. That it's the result of American ingenuity. Credit to a Frenchman, but Made in America." Miss Ruth nodded. "And, my mom made the moissanite story a life lesson. She said that it might seem at first that a meteor hitting the earth was pure destruction, but good things come of bad."

"You've stopped here. To find something good. A right ending for your story," Miss Ruth said.

"I guess."

Miss Ruth folded one old hand over the other. She shook her head. "People do all kinds of things to end their stories. Wasteful things like throwing rings into rivers —or craters. Or worse, throw away themselves. Last January a truck driver took it into his head to jump into a 100-foot mineshaft down by the crater. He lived, thank God. What are people thinking? Dust to dust?"

"Yes," Cole reddened.

"Well, they're feeling more than thinking." Miss Ruth motioned for Cole to hand her over a three-ringed binder full of photos.

Carol stood up to go. "I'd better get Drew. Cole, I'm so sorry."

"Thank you." He stood to help Carol pick up the cups and watched her exit. Then he sat down again. "Things crash and burn and life goes on. I don't want this ring to be about the crash and burn part."

"I hear you," said Miss Ruth.

"I want it to be about the diamonds out of the ashes story. A star plummeted to earth, and a man found something good in that. A way to make the star still shine, my mother said."

Miss Ruth's deep brown eyes riveted onto his and she began to make a pitch, "Cole, in 2005, Clement stumbled on this town and my sign in a daze after Hurricane Katrina took his home and family. He stayed and now we have a business. He cuts hair and together we transform heartache. I get most of our needy clients now from him. They tell him their stories. Most of our donors come in off the open road like you."

"Donors?"

"Clement says people don't get what they don't pay for. He means 'get' as understand." Miss Ruth chuckled, "He means 'get' as in 'obtain,' too. Clement can't help himself trying to be clever."

"So, you did this before Clement? How did you start to..."

"Transform heartache?" Miss Ruth reached for a framed black and white photo of a strapping handsome black man doffing a striped railroad cap and holding a lantern like the one at Miss Ruth's side.

"My husband Earl Lyons." Miss Ruth chuckled again, "Clement's a bit of a big city ad man. He suggested I change my name to De Leonne. Exotic for business, he said."

Miss Ruth rocked in her chair, "On Christmas Eve, 1940, my Earl was signalman at the railroad crossing by Somer's pass. He stood his ground to warn away from a moving train a young man determined, unbeknownst to my Earl, to end his life." Miss Ruth closed her eyes. "God must have blinked because that young man lived and my Earl died."

Cole returned the photo to Miss Ruth. "I'm sorry for your loss." She settled the photo down onto the table. "I trust God doesn't blink, but I struggled—I struggled—to find a purpose for my empty life. I prayed that God would help me to help especially young men and women find a better way to deal with heartache." Miss Ruth rubbed her hands over her lap to smooth the quilt. "At first when I hung my sign I was just a listener. For years, I prayed over folks in the boarding house where I lived and worked as a housekeeper. Clement said after Katrina he needed a listener so bad he almost started drinking so he could go to the AA. But he saw my sign. Clement settled down here, opened his shop and offered me my apartment. I was getting too old to do housework." Miss Ruth smoothed her quilt. "Clement helped a crazy old lady help people."

"Not crazy."

"Hah, Love makes you a little crazy, but it's a good crazy." Miss Ruth reached for and opened the black binder on her lap. "Let me explain how this system works, Cole. Look through this collection. Urgent cases have a red dot sticker."

Cole smelled a rat named Clement in all this "system" talk, but he surveyed the pages of photos tagged with short descriptions of the "clients" situations. Carol and her son Drew's page had a red sticker.

"Are there that many people wanting to 'donate?'"

"What donors get is the satisfaction that their loss, instead of being useless and painful will be a needy somebody's salvation." Cole pictured the old woman as a used car salesman in disguise delivering a sales pitch coached by Clement, he was certain. "Do you see someone you would like to help?"

Cole had flipped past and gone back to Carol and Drew's photo. "What's her story?"

"I thought so. I hoped so. I will pray so. Her situation's been upgraded to extremely urgent. In fact, she and her son are on site—Homeless. There are two extra bedrooms here. When we deem it safe and necessary those are rented to clients. There are several other clients downstairs with Clement. Carol and Drew are the ones onsite right now. Others drop in to talk, look for work in town, or talk to donors like you about their needs. Time for you to go on down. I need a nap. Clement will help out." Her extreme tiredness dawned on her as soon as she handed him the binder, Cole observed. Miss Ruth reached out her arms to hug him and Cole leaning over obliged. "Remember, Cole, helping others is a gift to God. Hurting others or yourself is tonic for the Devil."

"Yes, Ma'am."

Cole went back down the stairs, around to the barber store front and inside. Everybody looked anxious. Four adults and the child were still sitting in the waiting chairs. The truck driver and the truck was gone. Cole wondered if he was the one who survived the mineshaft jump last January. Cole felt himself among a crazy quilt community of sorts.

Clement asked each customer to tell Cole the story of why they had stopped at Miss Ruth's. "This young man is a donor."

Cole felt pushed from seeker to this donor role, but Carol and Miss Ruth seemed genuine even if Clement didn't. Cole's crook radar beeped ominously in his brain. A good Route 66 surname for Clement would be "Scalawag."

"Introduce yourselves," Clement continued. "Open your trapdoor and make your case."

A young collared priest, introducing himself as Father Joaquin, explained that he was collecting funds for his new church on an Indian reservation. After his haircut, he'd be visiting parishioners in a local hospital. "But Please, I just found out that this man has eleven children." He indicated a middle-aged man in a cowboy hat sitting beside him.

"Oh, Father. I'm just hanging around to find work," the cowboy said. "I'm good. My kids have jobs or they're still in school We're all good." He extended his hand to Cole. "Jess Kenner, my pleasure."

Cole looked at the next one, a man in a business suit who kept his head down and croaked in a raspy voice, "I have no health insurance and I need an operation."

Carol sat with her arm around Drew, who sported a too short spiky haircut. When it was her turn to speak, she seemed embarrassed. "Well, Drew's dad left. I have no family here. I'd like to get to my sister's in Cincinnati, Ohio."

Cole already had decided that they would receive his help and the ring. He indicated that she and the boy were his selection and was surprised when she refused. "No thank you," she said. Cole noticed that as she said that the boy looked at the croaking man in the suit who kept his head down.

"What's going on?" Cole asked.

"He needs the money. For an operation," Carol said. The boy then looked imploringly at his mother.

"I want to help you." Cole insisted.

"No, please. Give it to him," she tightened her grip on her son.

Cole glanced at the hoarse, suited sulker, then stared so long that the man fidgeted. As soon as Cole looked away and back to the young woman and boy the man folded his newspaper and got up. A map slipped out of his folded newspaper onto expensive red and black Nikes- the diner thief in his running away shoes!

Cole took one step in his direction. The man yanked open the shop door, exited, and bolted.

"Did he threaten you?" Cole asked Carol. "That guy tried to rob me at the Hashknife."

"Just a bad feeling," Carol said. "I have to be careful with Drew."

"There's bad seeds in every crop," Clement said quickly.

Carol glared at Clement.

"What's your last name? Do you have a plan now?" Cole questioned Carol.

"Carol Grant—and Drew. We do. We'll buy bus tickets to Cincinnati where my sister's made a place for us."

"How much for tickets?" Cole was counting out cash.

"What?"

"I want you to help you. And him. Please. I can afford it. How much more? And I want you to keep this ring for him…" He pulled the ring from his wallet. "… for when he gets married. To the right one. My mother would like that."

Carol kept looking at Clement. She had already figured the exact cost, which she stated to Cole. Cole gave her cash and the ring, which made her cry.

"Where's the bus station? I have to get back from leave soon," Cole said.

"I'll see she gets there, Brother, fine as silk, not to worry any at all." Clement said.

Cole lifted out his cell phone. "I'll call a taxi. Can you get ready that fast?"

"I'm ready," Carol said. "I'll get our suitcase and say goodbye to Miss Ruth." She grabbed Drew's T shirt at the shoulder and hurried him toward the outside stairs.

"For $20 my van's a taxi," Jess, the father of eleven, said, getting up from the red leather chair all the time avoiding Clement's harsh stare.

Cole said, "Good. I'd like to see them off."

"That won't be needed or necessary," Clement said. But Jess left anyway. When he pulled the van around to the front of the store, he got out and threw open the side door. Carol and Drew emerging from Miss Ruth's room with a suitcase, paused to make sure that Cole was coming along, then stepped up and into the van crossing in front of Clement now hovering outside with his arms extended like a scarecrow but still holding an open pair of scissors. He made to hug them goodbye, but Carol avoided him and only waved sideways to be polite.

"Does Aunt Sally have cable?" Drew asked his mom

as she buckled him in.

"She has an extra bedroom, and she loves us," Carol said and buckled in herself.

Cole, sensing that Carol was anxious to get away, shut the side door, moved into the shotgun seat, and they were off. Jess was prepared to drop Carol and Drew to catch the bus at the Interstate 40 rest stop because that was closest, but Cole gave him $10 more to take them directly to the bus station. "They might run into that damn thief."

"Thank you," Carol said. "I'm glad to stay far away from him. I got a weird vibe."

At the station, Carol bought tickets for a bus leaving for Cincinnati in half an hour. Cole helped her call her sister on his cell phone. When the time came for them to part, Carol seemed hesitant and glanced over at Jess more than once. Finally, she pecked Cole on the cheek and hugged him. "I wanted to hug you before," she said and turned away before Cole could respond. Carol and Drew waving goodbye from within the fogged bus window would be stamped on his mind forever.

Back in the van, Jess didn't say a word at first. "Good you saw to it that she left," he said finally. "Clement's been making promises and then threats to keep her paying rent over there. She and the boy bring in a lot."

"What are you talking about?"

"People sympathize with a single mom." He drove Cole back to the barber shop. Cole was glad to see his bike still there. Clement came right up to the van and hustled Jess inside to have words with him.

"Hey, Clement," Cole called to the crooked barber who looked over. "Swallows."

"What?"

"Swallows return to Capistrano, not fish." Clement, dazed for a second, his face a frozen mask of anger, waved Cole off, and resumed his fussing at Jess.

Cole mounted his cycle and circled back to the Interstate, his leave time ticking away.

Cole had ridden about 10 miles thinking maybe he shouldn't have given up his mother's ring, that his favorite material connection to his mother was lost forever, when his cell phone vibrated. He pulled over. It was Carol.

"Cole, remember the truck stop before Two Guns?"

"Yeah, Sure." Cole remembered it as the place he bypassed to go to the diner where he was almost robbed.

"Where are you?" Carol said. "Could you meet us there? We have a 10-minute rest stop."

"I could, I just passed it, but what's the matter? What happened?"

"I have to tell you in person. Please. Hurry."

Cole found Carol and the boy waiting by their bus, the motor of which was idling and churning fumes.

"What's the matter?" Cole asked.

"I won't take your ring," Carol said holding out her hand. "It's your mother's. You keep it." She put the ring into his hand and folded his fingers over it. "Thank you for the ticket. I'll pay you back. I know you're Army. I've got your cell number. But I won't keep the ring."

"Keep it for him I said."

"No, I won't. It belongs to you. From your mother, Cole. Drew and I are safe. That's all we need." People were beginning to re-board the bus. She added quickly, "I was afraid if I didn't take it, you'd give it to Clement—or Jess. Jess's an employee kind of. Of Clement's. Clement gives some of the "donations" away, but not everything. He uses needy people like Jess—and milks tourists. And I'm pretty sure he works a deal with the guy who tried to rob you.

He's at the shop all the time. Always has a new sob story. I may have been paranoid, but I felt that he would take Drew. Anyway, your ring's just booty to them. If I took anything from you and you left, they'd have demanded it of me. Clement does give Miss Ruth a place to live. He uses her, too, though. What choice does she have? She just says nobody's perfect. Nobody's perfect. Clement didn't lose his family in Katrina. That's bullshit. Clement's a fake. Miss Ruth's the real deal—like you, Cole." Carol put her hands on Cole's shoulders, kissed him briskly on the mouth, and turned toward the bus. The boy was already climbing aboard.

Cole grabbed her arm, turned her around and kissed her again. A molten current of vibrant joy fired through the atmosphere of his grief astonishing him. Carol pulled away laughing. "I have to go." She touched his face. "Cole, I have to go."

"I'll text your sister my number," he said.

"She has it, silly. How'd you think I called you? I borrowed a cell phone from a lady on the bus and called my sister for your number. I told her to save it."

"You'll call me?"

"I will," she said and turned to climb aboard.

Shaken, Cole watched the bus drive away. Again. But this time with hope. His mother's ring, shining in the sun, slid onto his little finger like a hug. Cole climbed onto the cycle and headed east. He had 48 hours to report to base.

Back at the barber shop Jess and Clement argued about the ring and money and tenants that got away and about who's supposed to get what share of valuable donations. "It's a business. My business," Clement argued.

In her room upstairs, Miss Ruth raised herself up from prayers, bent over to extinguish her lantern, clicked on the monitor long enough to learn from Jess and Clement's bickering that Carol was indeed on a bus to her sister's, then clicked it off to rest. "Good things come from bad," she said. "Good things come from bad."

Rings

Brandon and Zee, both active duty U. S. Army servicemen, had agreed between themselves to deposit a ring with a trustworthy person who resided or worked in a town that lay as near to the middle of their two bases as possible. Neither had leave time to spare, neither wanted to trust the postal service to be able to locate the other in these times of faraway wars. Both, especially since they were combat stress tested, valued their own and the other's ability to discern who in any group of persons was trustworthy, reliable, and most likely to complete the mission of safeguarding and exchanging the ring. Modern technology made it easy to communicate with one another, for Zee to message Brandon that he was preparing to propose to his fiancée, but even the slickest technology couldn't give them more time to plan a meeting, so they made a plan.

Brandon Parry rode up and down the main street of a little town named Promise looking for a local flea market, which a gas station attendant had told him was renowned statewide. For the purpose of depositing the ring with someone, the name of the town appealed to Brandon, and if the flea market was known across the state chances are his friend, Zee, might at least be able to find it. Brandon chose the town of Promise, as well, because of its easy access. The town was close enough to the interstate to experience a sound track of traffic noise on busy travel days. This morning, Brandon was very hungry, but determined to find the flea market before he had to leave to begin classes. He made another pass down the avenue and realized that an old Victorian Firehouse wasn't a fire station anymore.

The flea market on both floors of the impressive brick building wasn't open yet so Brandon yielded to the gnarling hunger pangs pushing him toward the town diner. He'd read in a magazine story that whole American diners were being disassembled, sold, and shipped to France to lovers of Americana. Some grace or will had left this metal marvel intact and buzzing with early morning activity.

Mary, her graying auburn hair restrained in a tidy bun by a single chopstick, wiped the grill in back to the tune "Ain't Too Proud to Beg" on an oldies station. She carried a hot white rag across and in and out of grooves in the metal grill, then vaulted the stained rag into a wash bucket. She noted Brandon's arrival, washed her hands at the cook sink, hooked a clean hot mug on her thumb and walked toward the coffee station behind the counter in the front of the house. "Coffee honey?" She filled the mug.

Brandon nodded, then eased the numbness of his fingers and lips by nestling the fevered mug; only after this centering pause did he shake open a sugar, pour in cream from a tiny handleless porcelain pitcher and stir. Mary stood by thinking: soldier, short hair.

"Thank you, Ma'am." Polite.

"Breakfast?"

"Soon." Resolute.

"Just say Mary." Mary resumed her clean up routine, her attention percolating into the vacuum of Brandon's aloneness. So, before he asked, she refilled his mug. "What'll it be, son?"

"Thank you. Three eggs scrambled. Hash browns. Rye toast."

"Meat?"

"What? Thank you, no."

Brandon strained unsuccessfully to read the wristwatch on the man beside him at the counter who rustled a concealing tent of newspaper. "Mary?" Brandon said. Mary turned pen in hand. "Do you know what time the flea market opens?"

She slipped the pen behind her ear. "The Antique Mall?"

"Yes."

Mary snapped her fingers against the tent of newspaper. "Casey, what time do you open up officially over there?"

Casey didn't lower the paper. "Eight—to customers."

Mary leaned closer to Brandon. "Most of the guys

in here right now are venders. They'll get up to leave around 7, 7:30. Doors open at 8."

"No early birds," said the newspaper.

Mary winked. Brandon lifted his chin and nodded. "You've got time to kill," Mary said.

"I guess I do."

Mary called in the order to Davis, the short order cook. In a few moments, she slid his plate of fragrant food in front of Brandon. "What are you shopping for, Son?"

"Shopping? Oh, I'm not shopping. I have a ring to maybe---sell." He was, in a sense, delivering it, certainly not selling it, but that was hard to explain.

"Ah." Mary sensed the brakes drawn. Break up maybe, she figured.

"Yo, Mary," a customer called from a booth.

As Mary turned away, the newspaper tent flopped down. "You got a ring to sell."

"Could be."

"Let me see it," Casey the vender said as if he'd be doing Brandon a favor.

Brandon hesitated, but two fingered a royal blue velvet box from a pocket in his T- shirt, thumbed a pearl release, drew the ring from a satin base and handed it to Casey.

Casey retrieved a jeweler's loupe from his pocket and eyed the ring. "I'll give you $150.00, and you don't have to hang around." He didn't hand the ring back.

Brandon reached for his ring. "No thanks."

Casey closed his fingers over it. "Two hundred right now."

Brandon's open hand waited. "That's OK. No."

"Do you want to sell the thing or not?" Casey held his fist tightly closed above Brandon's open palm.

"No. Thanks, Casey," Brandon said. Casey dumped the ring in Brandon's hand.

"You military?" Not waiting for an answer, "Do you have any combat stuff to sell? Helmets? I'm after one of those desert helmets."

"No helmets." Brandon gingerly replaced the ring in the antique blue box. Mary, returning to the counter, pretended not paying attention as Casey pushed money for his breakfast toward her, rolled up his paper, snapped it against the counter and headed for the door. "Don't waste my time then."

Mary moved toward Brandon, "What's your name son?"

"Brandon, Ma'am."

"Brandon. Look. Pretty much all these guys are venders." She swept up Casey's cash.

A thin man with desperate eyes waved enthusiastically like a child from a seat further down the counter.

"Not him. That's just Jasper."

"Is he drunk?"

"No, he's here for company. He's just…Jasper. He's here all the time. When they're gone, the venders…" She watched Brandon's face. "…I'll have time for a break before my Granddaughter picks me up. When the new shift comes in. We could talk." Mary wanted to hear Brandon's story. "I've been here since midnight." Brandon hadn't looked at her. "Not that I'm bragging or complaining."

"Sure, Ma'am. OK." Brandon put his toast on his bigger plate, picked up his coffee and followed the lead of Mary's extended hand to a vacant booth by the window from which he could see his parked cycle. He finished before Mary was finished her shift, putting his own dishes into a noisy heap which Mary cleared at one go returning with a steaming towel to swipe the worn, bleached pale surface. "What's that smell?"

"Oh, I pepper table rags with lavender oil. It's supposed to have relaxing properties my Granddaughter tells me. Makes me feel careful."

Brandon breathed coffee, lavender oil and bacon on the grill. On the road today scents of green grass and pine shot through him like exploding time capsules that whisked him home.

Soon Mary sans apron and having put on a purple sweater rattled her tea cup to the table and slid in the other side of the booth. Sitting was a pain reliever. "Oh, I forgot the honey."

"Hey, I got it." Brandon followed her gaze and brought her two plastic pack honey portions from the counter.

"Bless you and your young self." She peeled back the foil and let honey ooze into her tea. "So tell me your ring story."

"This is a friend's. Well, it was."

"You a soldier? Iraq?"

"And Afghanistan." Brandon raised his coffee cup

with two hands and put it down in the same place. He knew he didn't want to ask the likes of Casey to guard the ring. He was considering asking Mary.

"Are you going back?"

"I been back, Ma'am. Seven times. Time to move forward with my life."

"Seven tours?"

"No use talking about that. I'm from around here basically-East Coast, but I have a friend in upstate New York. He talked me into going back to school in the city."

"What do you want to do with the ring?"

"I don't want to sell it."

"I can see that. You soured Casey's day. He lives to score a steal."

"I want my friend to have it to get engaged."

"Where's your friend.?" Mary sipped her tea.

"A ways north of here. Fort Drum." He opened the box to display the ring to Mary.

Mary had no engagement ring; her wedding band was her mother's. "That's beautiful," meaning his intention to deliver the ring to his friend.

Brandon was quiet.

Rings

"Two of us fought in infantry together. Me and JT. This other friend, Zee, his proper name is Zorawar, is a dentist. At Fort Drum now. We used to talk. The ring belonged to JT's mom. JT made a pact with us that the first to get engaged would use the ring. JT was pretty sure it was going to be him. Then he got killed. He had left me the ring for safe keeping. Zorawar, Zee, is about to get engaged. JT would want him to have the ring. I want that, too."

Mary nervously fingered the ring she was wearing.

"What's the story of your ring? Where did your husband get it?"

"Mine's a war bride who wasn't story."

"What?"

"This is my mother's ring. She passed away. I was kind of married. I wear it now, I guess, to appear married. I feel that I should have been."

"But you have a granddaughter."

"Aren't you sharp?" Mary continued. "My fiancé, I guess it's fair to call him that, died in a helicopter crash in Viet Nam. I got the news from his sister on the same day that I thought I might be pregnant. I thought I felt ill from the shock of hearing he was dead. No. I was pregnant."

"I'm sorry. I mean…"

"I had my daughter. My greatest blessing. Funny. She hasn't married either. She had an affair she called 'a heart attack.'"

"But,"

"Yes. She also found herself pregnant. Her baby's father had a ring already, so did his wife. We form a long line of ring debits." Mary sipped her tea. "My daughter at least finished college. She's a nurse. Her daughter's the love of both our lives. Now I'm bragging. You'll meet her when she picks me up."

"What's she studying?"

"Medical School. Her mother told her if you want to be a nurse, you may as well become a doctor."

"Good plan."

"Yeah. Say, if you really trust me to, I'll wear your ring until your friend comes to pick it up."

"Are you reading my mind?"

"That would save you the trip up to Fort Drum. That's practically Canada, and good road weather isn't guaranteed this time of year. Lend me your ring to wear.

Rings

I meet a lot of people. I like to get a reaction. Hear what people have to say. It'd be fun. Believe me a lot of people'll ask an old lady why she's all of a sudden wearing an engagement ring."

Brandon looked at the ring. He considered Mary a good prospect, but he was quiet to emphasize how important this was for him.

Mary laid her full hand on the table. "I haven't sold my mother's ring. I'm not going to sell your ring. You don't want to sell it." Brandon shook his head. "Or give it over to someone like Casey." Brandon shook his head again. "Lend it to me. Have your friend pick it up when he can. You can trust me." Mary sat back against the booth. "Frankly, I trust me with the ring more than you seeing as you already tempted Casey with it."

They laughed.

A young girl with auburn hair drove into the parking lot in a dusty red Focus and parked next to Brandon's cycle.

"I'd give it to you if I could." Brandon nodded toward the girl. "Your granddaughter must need money for med school."

"Yeah, that's her. We don't need money. She's smart. See what I mean about not trusting you with the ring. Here you are ready to give it away when a whole lot of people, especially these low days, could use your friendship story."

Brandon flushed.

Upon entering the diner, Mary's granddaughter looked around by the cash register, spotted the back of Mary's chopsticked hair, and headed for the booth.

Brandon was facing her, "She's pretty."

"She's smart."

"OK." Brandon handed the ring over to Mary who slipped it onto her finger above her mother's wedding band.

"What's going on?" Mary's granddaughter said too loudly.

Mary winked at Brandon. "See? People are interested." To her granddaughter, she said, "I'm borrowing this ring."

"Why?"

"Brandon, here is going back to school. In New York City. And he needs somebody to mind the ring. Someone who's careful with things and people."

Rings

"You picked a winner." Mary's granddaughter pushed in beside her.

When Mary borrowed the ring from Brandon that day, she just wanted to keep him from handing it over to the wrong person. As it turned out, in the weeks and months to come, the ring on Mary's finger triggered stories from customers who, though they had been stopping in daily for years, had never said a word beyond, "Any more cream?" and from travelers seeking the roadside comfort of familiar expectations and a hospitable word in a day or days of sterile driving on the Interstate. Slipping the shine of a beautiful ring on her aging hands had the effect of lighting a welcome candle to conversation.

One shy portly man, a vender, inquired about the new ring Mary wore. "You meet somebody?" Mary told Brandon's story. The man said, "I used to wear my wife's wedding band after she passed. On my little finger." He turned it empty in the air.

"So, where's the ring?" Mary asked. The man explained that as he gained weight in his advancing years because his wife wasn't around to monitor his snacking habits, the ring started to pinch. One day while waiting for a train, he struggled the ring from his finger, placed it on the bench beside him, and said a prayer to his wife, asking if it was okay with her if he didn't wear it anymore. He started to get emotional then and struggled to hide tears from other commuters waiting at the train station. By accident, when the train arrived, "like the old fart that I am, I left the ring on the bench." He searched for it later to no avail. But, he said the best part of the story, was that when he told his daughter about the missing ring, instead of being angry with him, his daughter said "Mom took it back to heaven."

An elderly woman whose daughter "carried me out shopping today" flashed at Mary the engagement ring her husband had given her for their 34th wedding anniversary when "we could finally afford one."

"You want to find rings," Casey the cranky vendor boasted one morning. "It's easy. These days' metal detectors show the image of what's just beneath the surface. You want to see a ring? Go to the beach. I average maybe ten a summer."

Ten lost stories Mary thought.

A lady told of losing the diamond from her engagement ring. "Just dropped out. Who knew where?" One day, "had to be years later, a gloomy day," she lit a fire in her fireplace. "I thought a live ember had jumped to a knot in the wood floor, so I went at it with a wet paper towel and into my palm rolls the diamond. What're the odds it could dodge the vacuum cleaner?"

"Higher at my house," Mary said.

One man found a diamond in a bird's nest. "No dumb bird," Mary said.

That man's story prompted Casey to drop his newspaper and bark, "Come on, what bird puts a diamond in its nest?"

"Crows," the other man said. "It's a known fact that crows lift shiny items like gold chains and loose change and like the diamond into their nests."

"Loose change, come on." Casey retreated flapping open his newspaper tent with a grunt, but Mary imagined he'd be paying a lot more attention to crows.

Another man told how he couldn't cheer up his wife when she misplaced her diamond ring, so to clear his head he went outside to burn the trash. "You could burn your own trash in those days." Afterwards, he raked the ashes to extinguish the fire and his wife's ring caught on a tine of the rake. "She had a habit of balling it up in tissue when she did dishes." He cleaned the ring, put it in a gift box and gave it back to her on their anniversary. "I scored big time. She said it was her favorite gift—ever."

One day a young couple, the boy blond, the girl Japanese, stopped into the diner from off the Interstate. The couple sat together on one side of a booth. Mary noticed that they kept looking at the girl's ring and turning it on her finger.

"Are you engaged?"

"Just," the boy said." Her father said 'yes.'"

"Her father?"

The girl beckoned for Mary to join them in the booth. "I'll hear your story at dessert." Mary said. When she brought them the check, she sat down. "OK, tell me."

"I made a video…" the boy began.

"In Japanese," the girl said grinning.

"… to ask her father for permission to marry his daughter. He called us yesterday evening on the cell and said 'Yes.' Since Japan is thirteen hours ahead, we wanted to wait till after he had officially given us his blessing. At the thirteenth hour mark we were at a bridge, so we pulled over and I asked her to marry me."

"In English," the girl said. They looked at each other.

"She said 'yes,' too."

"Some bridge," said Mary. "How'd you meet?"

"My company videoed her hula class in Brooklyn."

"God bless America," Mary said.

One slow rainy day Jasper sat by Mary as she worked a crossword puzzle. Raindrops coursed down the windows. "That's nice," Jasper said.

Mary looked at her ring. "Yeah. Thanks Jasper."

"I mean that you do crosswords."

"Oh, yeah."

"My mother did them. She said they increased brain power, which is important in this world."

"She still does them?"

"She passed away."

"Sorry."

"Anyhow, I haven't seen her since I was nine."

Mary straightened up. "Nine? It's hard for a kid to lose a mother."

"She didn't pass away then... I got sent to the state home."

Mary looked at Jasper as if for the first time. "Even though you had your mom?"

"My dad left us. In those days if a parent couldn't take care of kids and the state got wind of it, they'd put you in the state home. She had some kind of breakdown after my dad left. I got out at 18."

Suddenly Jasper made sense to Mary; he was history, one of the state institution kids of the 50s and 60s. He hadn't learned the social graces. Jasper interrupted people. He often spoke to himself in parallel to a patron. He craved social contact, but didn't know how to get it. He was like a fighter walking all around the ring, fists working, sometimes striking out wildly, not expecting to be engaged. Yanked from his mother in a fatherless home, Jasper was shelved in an institution where each aspect of life: sleeping, eating, schooling, working was programmed not to require his participation as an individual, even to discourage his participation, encouraging only a manageable group identity.

"You're the first state kid I ever met up close."

Rings

Jasper bowed. "Yeah? Anyhow, I have a ring, too." He pulled from under his shirt a knotted leather lace, at the bottom hung a woman's engagement ring.

"Pretty." Mary turned it in her hands. "You bought it for someone?"

"No. It's from my mom. They took me to her funeral and after took me to a lawyer's office. He gave me the ring in a brown envelope. He said she had left a will saying that the ring should be mine. While I opened the envelope, he said that there was no wedding ring. That maybe she was buried with it. I could call the funeral home if I wanted. I thought, no, she should keep it." Jasper tucked the ring back into his shirt. "I can't wear a lady's ring like a ring."

One Saturday, soon after hearing Jasper's story, Mary worked the later shift serving customers of the flea market who came in for lunch. That day Mary got to meet and talk to the flea market duchess, as the lunch shift described Lydia Chestnut-Billings, an authentic Philadelphia blue blood. Lydia attended without fail every weekend, her purchases filling at least three paper shopping bags which she brought in from the likes of Saks, Lord and Taylor, and Neiman Marcus. Rumor was that she was a clutter bug who made purchases for no other reason than to satisfy her every fancy. Mary learned that, in fact, she made as many trips to shelters to donate reading lamps, coats, and quilts. Lydia Chestnut-Billings would order hot tea with lemon and a scrapple sandwich on wheat toast with a poached egg on top. Davis, the cook, kept one piece of toast ready with a hole cut out of the middle to receive her egg. Somewhat intimidated, none of the other waitresses conversed with her, but Lydia, intrigued by Mary's ring initiated conversation.

"Darling," Lydia cooed in Lauren Bacall tones, "who put that tasty ring on your finger, and how did he get past me?" Mary told Brandon the soldier's story and Lydia Chesnut-Billings, with some prodding relayed one of her own.

"It's a dirty story." She pulled off velvet gloves and folded them into her purse. Although her wrists were arrayed with gold bangles, she wasn't wearing any rings. "I was marketing my estate after the D-I-V-O-R-C-E, and a potential buyer wanted me to clean the gate house septic system. In its entire history, mind you, the gatehouse had

Rings

only had two occupant caretakers, both single men. But, all right, so I hired a company, and happened to mention that I had lost a $3,000 engagement ring down the drain years ago when I first met my ex and we—rendezvoused—at the gatehouse. The company must have had a filter on their pump because apparently, they 'unearthed' my ring.. I say apparently because they didn't tell me about it. Say, I'm parched."

Mary poured Lydia a glass of ice water with a lemon slice.

"Thanks, my dear." Lydia squeezed the lemon and took a long drink. "At a lady friend's house for lunch some weeks later, my friend said her daughter's boyfriend, a plumber, had asked her daughter to marry him and gave her an 'enormous' ring. I said wouldn't I love to see it. The Mom called in the daughter who turned her finger in a ray of sunlight to especially display for me the shine. I asked the name of her fiancé. You guessed it." Lydia waved a bejeweled wrist and manicured hand. "I couldn't soil her dream. I like the girl, and I love my friend, her mother. They'll never know. Unless you tell." Mary shook her head. Jasper did too. Lydia looked twice at Jasper. He shook his head more vehemently. "I never did sell the place. The gatehouse stands empty." Lydia enjoyed talking with Mary, and she started to come in earlier on Mary's shift. Eventually, after their friendship matured, Mary told Lydia about Jasper and how he was living in one room at a seedy boarding house. Lydia and Mary convinced Jasper to move into Lydia's gate house to be caretaker assuring him that he could still visit at the diner.

When the weather warmed up, Mary's radar had only begun to quicken in expectation of Brandon's friend ever picking up the ring when a man entered the diner one Saturday morning. Mary looked up because the buzz of conversation ceased. She looked into the onyx eyes of a man wearing a plaid shirt, jeans, and a turban. The man walked toward her and took a seat at the counter next to Casey who was, as usual, oblivious behind his tent of newspaper.

Mary handed the gentleman a menu wondering if she was correct in presuming that he had sought her out. After only a brief glance at the menu, the man placed the menu on the counter.

"Breakfast?"

"Please for your bran muffin and a coffee, black."

"You got it."

"Thank you, Mary."

Mary turned back and paused.

"Yes, I'm a friend of Brandon's."

"Brandon sent you for the ring, right?" Mary's tone and question brought Casey from behind his tent of newspaper. He stared nonplussed.

"Brandon wanted me to meet you anyway, so we took this opportunity. I am attending a conference near here. My name is Zorawar Singh; I first met Brandon and JT as their language instructor slash dentist in Afghanistan."

"Afghanistan." Casey barked as if the word fitted a puzzle piece in his brain.

"Are you a soldier too?" Mary asked.

"On our side?" Casey glowered.

"Yes. And yes, of course. I was born in this country."

"Muslim?"

"Casey!"

"Sikh. Our friend Jabir, JT, practiced Islam. Many Muslims serve our country, which is their country, too. It's

JT's ring that you've been safekeeping, Mary. Thank you."

"Since when is that part of any U.S. Army uniform?" Casey gestured toward the turban.

"As a follower of Sikh precepts, I do not remove my turban. Not even to fight in war."

"You don't even wear a helmet?"

"A grand uncle of mine received the Victoria Cross fighting for the British army during World War II. He never wore a helmet. I do wear the helmet these days—adjusted over my turban."

"Victoria Cross. Christmas." Casey mumbled. Mary felt it was safe then to leave them and get the order. Casey, struggling on a high wire between discomfort and curiosity, then retreating into discomfort, slammed down some money, rolled up his newspaper, hit the counter, and started to exit, but turned around. "Stop over the firehouse. Vender 147. I have a lot of British World War II pieces."

"Not interested. I have very little time; I'll be driving on to Philadelphia. Have a good day and thank you, Sir."

Casey hit the newspaper roll against his hand in answer, and walked out.

Mary set down the coffee and muffin. "That's Casey

as friendly as it gets. You rocked his world. Your name is Zee?"

"My nickname. My proper name is Zorawar." Before starting to eat, he reached into his back pocket. "Oh, I have a letter from Brandon. He's quite busy with his business courses and exams." He unfolded a paper and handed it to Mary.

She read:

> "Dear Mary, Zee is the friend I told you who talked me into college. You can trust him with the ring. It's his now. I'll be by sometime, too. This summer. Promise I'll come to Promise. Remember me to your granddaughter.
>
> Peace, Brandon."

She folded the note into her apron and handed Zorawar her pen. "Kindly write down your full name for me? My brain sees better than it hears. How exactly did you meet Brandon?"

"Of course." Zorawar accepted Mary's pen, and she noticed a bracelet on his wrist. "Like Brandon, and JT, we wanted to serve our country after 9/11. I was contracted to Afghanistan since I spoke the language." He slipped a notebook from his shirt pocket, and wrote down his name. "Sikhs are a wandering people. My father, born in Afghanistan, emigrated to America. He spoke to me in Farsi of Kabul, a city he remembers as full of flowers and cooking smells." He handed Mary the paper and clasped his neat dark hands on the counter. "In our language class, to spark interest I told the story of the Koh-I-Noor, the magnificent diamond of Sikh lore that today adorns the royal crown in England. Brandon and JT asked a lot of questions, a lot of questions—and we all became friends." He patted his hands on the counter. "Most recently, Brandon attended my swearing in ceremony."

"To the Army?"

"Yes. At first, the U. S. Army disallowed the precepts of my faith. Brandon and others wrote persuasive letters on my behalf."

"Brandon's a good friend."

"A brother." He finished his coffee and stood. Mary started to pull the ring from her finger. "One moment. Brandon and I have a gift for you." He pushed back his sleeve to slip the metal bracelet from his wrist. "I planned to give this bracelet called a 'Kara' to Brandon for his help in getting me into the Army. He said to give it to you instead." Mary held out her right wrist. "Actually Mary, our Sikh tradition holds that women, in every way equally esteemed and revered, wear the Kara on their left wrist."

Mary made the switch, and Zorawar slid the Kara onto her wrist. "Brandon asked me if I would consider giving the Kara to you. It was your idea to safeguard the ring, he said."

"An honor, thank you. What does it say inside?"

"The inscription is a mantra. A prayer. This one means 'One universal God. No fear. No hatred. Unborn. Undying. True in the beginning. True now. True forever.'"

"Wow. Thank you."

Zorawar laughed. Mary slipped the ring from her finger, gave it a kiss, and handed it to Zorawar who fitted it into a small silk envelope. Brandon still had the blue box. "It's true I don't have a lot of time, Mary. My conference in Philadelphia has already begun."

"Will you see him soon?"

"I will. My conference is just north of Philadelphia. I'll stop to see Brandon in New York City on my way back." Zorawar stowed the enveloped ring in his shirt pocket.

He reached out to shake Mary's hand and she took his hands in both of hers. "What's she like?"

"My fiancée? Kind and beautiful. Like you."

Mary lowered her eyes, smiled, and looked at him again. "Her name?"

"Hardeep, it means 'light of God.'"

"So very good to meet you."

"Likewise."

Zorawar walked toward the door, all heads turning.

"Tell Brandon my granddaughter asks about him."

Zorawar Singh nodded and held open the door for Lydia the flea market duchess. Mary couldn't tell if Lydia's mouth or eyes opened wider as she sashayed her collection of yet empty shopping bags to an empty booth.

"If I'd known the king of Siam was making an appearance, I'd have been in earlier."

"He knows Brandon," said Jasper sitting at the bar. "He took the ring back."

Lydia looked at Mary's hand and saw for herself the ring was gone.

Mary nudged the bracelet. "He gave me this beautiful bracelet called a Kara."

"What's the whole story? Has Brandon gone and gotten engaged to a Muslim?"

"He's Sikh," said Jasper. "They didn't used to wear helmets, but they do now."

"Brandon sent Zorawar to pick up the ring because Zorawar's getting engaged. Brandon and Zorawar are good friends." Mary was used to speaking in between Jasper jabber.

"Helmet? Looked like a turban to me. You gave this man the ring?"

"Yes," Mary repeated. "He's a good friend of Brandon's."

"Brandon sent a letter. He's coming this summer." Jasper offered, "He can stay with me at the gatehouse."

"Surely Brandon's engaged to somebody by now. I admire his drama sense with the whole ring go round. I'd marry him myself."

"You don't know Brandon," Jasper cut in.

"Well, I like Brandon even so. I just wish such a nice young man could find somebody."

"He'll find somebody." Mary leaned over and waved

through the window to Zorawar who waved back as he got into his car. "He found all of us."

Lydia lifted Mary's hand. "People are going to ask what happened to your beautiful ring."

"Now she has a bigger ring," Jasper said.

Mary lifted the bracelet away from her wrist and read aloud the part of the inscription she could see, "True in the beginning. True now. True forever."

Acknowledgments

Thank you to my husband, Michael, for saying "I like when you write," and for believing that my writing is worthwhile even when I wondered. Thank you, as well, to my daughters, Carolyn and Kate for that same regard for creativity. May your art continue to deepen and enrich your lives. Thank you, Carolyn, for crafting the cover for this book. Thank you to my sister, Nan, and son-in- law, Duke, for being inciteful and patient readers on call. Thanks to all readers.

Thanks to writers, short story writers, in particular. Thanks to my writing friends, Jehane, Beth, Kim, Alex, Marian, Liz, Irene, KK, Mary, Ben, Rike and all the Wild Minds Writers. Thanks to Madison for first gathering us together in that Chinatown raw foods café that was ahead of its time. Thanks to dear friends, family and students far and near, present and past whose counsel and encouragement are golden. Thanks for the Sunday breakfast trip where I met author, Sinéad Tyrone, whose motto is "Dream no small dreams," and who told me about No Frills Buffalo. Thank you to Mark at No Frills Buffalo for helping me to publish this book. Thank you to my granddaughter Zoe for being.

Works Referenced

Bridges, Robert, from The Testament of Beauty, Poetry for the Spirit, edited by Alan Jacobs, Barnes and Noble Inc., 2002.

charlesandcolvard.com/company/the-charles-colvard-story/, ©2017. Date accessed March 2017.

Cohen, Leonard. "Last Year's Man," The Best of Leonard Cohen, CBS Records, 1975.

"Gems, Forms of Cutting," Rafal Swiecki, Geological Engineer, www.minelinks/alluvial/plate2.html. Posted in the Public Domain, March, 2011. Date accessed March, 2017.

Johnson, O.W., quoted by Tom Marshall, in "Plovers Tracked Across the Pacific,"www.phys.org/news, Provided by PlanetEarth Online, Posted June 13, 2011. Date accessed January 2013.

McKay, Claude. Selected Poems, published June, 1999, by Dover Publications (first published April 1969).

nobelprize.org/nobel_prizes/chemistry/laureates/1906/Moissan-bio, Henri Moissan Biography from Nobel Lectures, Chemistry 1901-1921, Elsevier Publishing Company, Amsterdam, 1966. This autobiography was written at the time of the award of the Nobel Prize and first published in the book series Les Prix Nobel. It was later edited and republished in Nobel Lectures. Date accessed March 2017.

Wallis, Michael. Route 66: The Mother Road, St. Martin's Griffin, June 23, 2001.

"Warrior Saint~Captain Tejdeep Singh Rattan~a Sequel," Stephanie Gottschich, webapp2.wright.edu, Fall 2010 issue of Wright State University Magazine. Date accessed April 2013.

Made in the USA
Columbia, SC
07 September 2017